SOARING

VERONICA MULL

First Edition

Written by Veronica Mull
Edited by Laura Wilkinson
Cover by Damon Biddle
Publishing Assistance by V. L. Dreyer

DEDICATION

This book is dedicated to my two sons Xzavier and Edward, my daughter baby Rose, my mother Rhonda Turner and my late father A.G. Turner a.k.a fattie.

PREFACE

CRYSTAL

Sometimes, life doesn't go as planned. This is something
I've learned growing up in Bay City.

PETER

All because of a girl.

CHAPTER 1

"Crystal, so are you coming to my party today?" My cousin Patrick asked me, we always call him Pat. I wasn't sure if I could be bothered as I knew his annoying friend Peter would be there, and Peter always asks me a ton of questions. I hate it when Peter says anything to me, but Pat knew my older brother and sister would be there, so I guess he's just making sure I'm also coming.

"Uh yea let me ask my mom first." I yelled and asked her if we can go, knowing she would say yea.

"Hello Pat, she said yea."

"Yes." His excitement was felt over the phone, so I couldn't help but to be excited with him.

"Well, ok see you later."

We hung up and I was left with the task of finding something to wear. I thought about just wearing a skirt or dress, but I knew I couldn't play like I usually would. I chose a pair of blue jeans and a yellow sweater. The clothes are very comfortable and my hair is pulled back in one puffy ponytail.

When I finished getting dressed, my sister Cherish and Brother Michael and I walked over to Pat's house which was like eight blocks over. The weather is nice, traffic is heavy, and we are parentless. Cherish held our hand every time we crossed the street, and she stood in the middle of us each time. My mom trusted her to keep us safe and she did exactly that until we made it to our destination.

We made it to our Auntie Cynthia's house; it is big with white paneling over it. Cherish knocked on the door. We heard a distant "who is it?" from the other side of the door. My auntie opens the door herself.

"Hey auntie's babies." I hated when she referred to us as babies. Really, us babies? No way, because Cherish is 18, Michael is 17, and I'm 15, we're far from babies.

"Hey auntie." We all said in unison.

"Come in, the other kids are in the basement playing and waiting for the food, and to sing happy birthday." Auntie informed us.

We passed her and headed straight to the basement door. Her house has so many stairs to go down just to get to the basement, but boy did we have our share of fun on these stairs. The stairs are wooden so you can hear every crack, and we couldn't sneak and say surprise because they heard us coming. I looked down to see Pat was at the bottom of the steps waiting for us. Pat was smiling so hard his smile was infectious, and made us smile. We all said happy birthday and gave him a hug.

We made it to the basement which was dim with strobe colorful lights. The lights are red, green, and blue just for a boy. The basement walls are covered in mirrors which is cool and useful. While being hugged, Pat smashed my pony tail, so I used the mirrors to fix my pony tail. When I was done, I felt a tap on my shoulder which made me look up, and there he is, Peter Jackson.

"Hey Crissy."

"Crystal is my name, and hi."

"Well you look like a Crissy to me."

I Let out a frustrated sigh and walked away to avoid any more conversation with Peter. I don't know why he irritated me so much. On the other side of the basement there was a basketball, so I picked it up and started to bounce it. Glancing Peter's way, thinking to myself *who does he think he is giving me a nickname?*

"Crystal, pass me the ball."

I looked up to see who asked for the ball and that's when I see Sarah and her sister Nicole. They are my auntie's neighbors, and I would only see them if I came over here. I honestly was shocked she is speaking to me, Sarah that is. When I first met Sarah we didn't get along too well, and she always had something negative to say and thought it was funny.

"Here, catch." I threw the ball, which caught Peter's attention.

"How about a game of dodge ball?" Peter asked with a playful smile.

Sarah and Nicole was all for it, but I didn't see the fun in being hit by a ball.

"Uh, no I'll pass." Seeing the disappointment on Peter's face when trying to walk away, he grabbed my hand and looked me dead in the face.

"Come on Crissy, it will be fun." As awkward as it felt with him touching me, I couldn't refuse.

"Okay." I gave in to his request.

We started playing and there was a lot of screaming and laughing filling the basement. When everyone else heard and saw the fun, they joined in. Bam, here it is a hit to my head that made me regret agreeing to play this stupid game. I fell and Peter is the first person by my side. When I opened my eyes, I realized I'm the laughing stock of the party. I'm embarrassed and I would have cried if Sarah and Nicole wasn't watching me attentively. Trying to gather my thoughts, Peter reached out his hand to help me up. I accepted his help by placing my hand in his.

"Thank you."

"Are you okay?"

"Yea, my head will be fine." I said softly rubbing my head. "I don't like the fact that your girlfriend was laughing at me."

I was trying to sound pitiful and take the attention off my embarrassing moment.

"Who, Sarah?" Sounding shocked.

Wait. Why do I care if Sarah is his girlfriend?

"Yes, Sarah who else?" Those words shot out my mouth before I knew it. Why was I so defensive or angry at the thought of Peter and Sarah? Why hasn't she stopped staring at us?

"Okay, that ball must have hit you harder than I thought, because I don't know what you are talking about."

"Well, she likes you."

"She likes me?" I repeated, sounding like a broken record.

"Yes Y O U, and she haven't stopped looking at you since you've been over here and it's starting to make me feel uncomfortable."

We both laughed. Over the noise, we heard my auntie's voice telling us it's time to eat and sing happy birthday.

"Come on Peter."

Sarah said grabbing his hand and pulling him towards the stairs. Peter never let go of my hand, so I'm being dragged also by Peter. Sarah wasn't so happy to see him holding my hand while going up the stairs. When we came around the adults, he dropped my hand which made me laugh, because I knew why he released me. We ate hot dogs, chips, cookies, and we drunk some pop. When everyone was done, we sung happy birthday. Pat is happy, and his cake is delicious. It is white, blue, and red on the outside, and yellow on the inside. While eating our cake, Peter asked me, "When we go back downstairs, will you dance with me?"

He tried to whisper but failed, because Sarah heard what he asked and she is furious. Sarah's emotions are being expressed on her face. I guess that's what she gets for eavesdropping, but before I could answer, he said,

"At least think about it before you say no?"

"Okay, I will think about it."

I answered his question not giving away too many emotions. My insides were screaming "yes, I'd love to dance with you", but I refuse to let him see it. He smiled and walked away from the table. I never danced with a boy before and yet, I feel excited. After he left, here comes double trouble Sarah and Nicole and sat next to me, boxing me in the middle of them. They stared at me before Sarah spoke.

"I heard Peter asked you to dance with him."

"Okay, you heard correctly and your point is?"

"It's just that he's musty and if you don't want to smell like a bag of onions, you wouldn't dance with Peter."

"Okay I'll keep that in mind, now if you will excuse me."

My words are sharp, low, and demanding. I meant what I said. While walking away towards the basement. I felt their eyes piercing my back. In the basement, I found everybody minding their own business. They are playing video games, playing with toys and Peter had turned up the radio. It was louder than before, but no one seems to care. *Oh my* goodness, *here comes Peter walking towards me. I can't dance with him. Many reasons came to my mind like I'm scared, I didn't know how to dance, and I am shy.*

"So are we dancing together?" He asked with his hands extended out to me.

My heart started to race, my palms started to sweat, and my knees feel weak.

With no answer, I reluctantly placed my hand in his and we danced. I honestly have no idea how I am dancing, so I guess I will just continue following Peter's lead. I am surprised I didn't step on his feet, not once. I've never been this close to a boy before other than family. My stomach felt weird and warm on the inside. Pushing myself back from Peter, he pulls me back even closer into him. I am now on his chest and I was able to hear the rhythm of his fast heartbeat. He whispered in my ear.

"I'm really glad you are okay and you agreed to dance with me."

I had no words, but just caught up in the moment. The music is soft and the lyrics are simple. 'Bobby Brown Roni was playing.' What am I doing? When is this song going to end? A lot of questions are riding in my brain like a surfer on a wave. I kept my composure on the outside for the whole dance. Not showing the feelings that I felt on the inside. The main feeling is excitement. When the song finally stopped, I was relieved. Peter gave me a long bear hug and I saw Sarah staring at us from behind. If looks could kill, Peter and I would be dead. Pulling away me from him placing his hands resting on my arms, he said,

"Thank you for the dance."

"No, thank you for dancing with me." I said with a brief smile.

"See, I'm really not that bad once you get to know me."

"Okay I'll keep that in mind."

Peter walked off and didn't look back. I thought nothing of it, however, I felt something start to change in me. Peter wasn't that annoying kid who is my cousin's best friend, but maybe he is becoming my Pete as much as I am his Crissy? The party was fun and now it's time to leave. Everybody said their goodbyes and it was time for us to take our journey. Peter and Pat trailed along with us down a few blocks over before they turned back around. After that day, I don't think I viewed Peter the same.

We made it back home, and I heard my mom on the phone telling somebody we made it back. I ran straight to my room and grabbed my journal. I felt I had so much to write. I had so much to share and I couldn't wait.

Dear Journal,
Today was a very interesting day. It was my cousin Pat's birthday and he had a party. I was hit with a ball in the head and I had my first dance with a boy named Peter. Cherish and Michael hadn't said anything on the way home

so I wasn't either. Now I'm back to my regular schedule program, my life that doesn't involve boys. Overall, today was a good day.

Writing usually makes me sleepy. I wanted to keep writing, but eventually giving into the heaviness of my eyes, it was a wrap. Waking up the next morning with my notebook resting on my chest. I brushed my teeth, washed my face, and I looked in the mirror realizing I slept with my clothes on. Looking in the mirror, flashes of yesterday at the party went through my head. Squinting while holding my head where the ball hit me. That was something I may not forget. It was Saturday morning and upstairs was quite. I figured everybody was downstairs watching TV or having breakfast at the table. Finally, making it downstairs my predictions are right some are watching TV and some are having breakfast. I Walked by saying my good mornings to everybody.

"Crystal's got a boyfriend."

My little sister Brittany says it left me feeling flushed inside and rolling my eyes. I knew I just walked in on a conversation that had something to do with me and I wasn't there to defend myself. Sitting at the table not knowing what to expect, I was ready to enjoy my breakfast. My mom cooked the best pancakes. If I could eat nothing else, I would have her famous pancakes.

"Good morning Sunshine."

"Hey momma, how are you feeling?" "I hear you had a pretty interesting day yesterday." She knew, and I don't know what to say. I mean what did she want me to say, or was there anything to say?

"Yea, you can say that."

"So is there anything you would like to tell me?"

"I was hit on the head with a ball yesterday and everybody laughed except Peter."

Why did I even bring up his name? I was really trying to

avoid the dance and him period. Nope leave it up to me to give her an invite to drill me about Peter.

"Peter did a lot of things I heard."

"Okay, is there something you want to tell me"? Sarcasm took over trying to get her to share what she already knew.

"Don't be a smart mouth, sunshine."

"Well would you rather my mouth be dumb?"

I see by her facial expression I'm pushing my limits. If I was going to come clean, now will be a good time. She reached over the table and popped me on the side of my head.

"Ouch mom."

"You better get talking Sunshine, and I mean now."

"Peter asked me to dance with him and I danced."

"Did he now?"

Sounding surprise, but I knew she knew. Michael couldn't hold water. I'm certain it wasn't Cherish who ratted me out.

"Mom, you already knew."

"You're right, but I wanted you to tell me and not Michael."

"But he didn't even give me a chance, and besides, it's not a big deal."

"Oh, really? Well let's see what your dad has to say about you dancing with a pissy tail boy."

"No momma, please don't tell him, let me first."

Placing my face in my hands forgetting the syrup that is on my hands. Thinking about two possible outcomes neither one I liked, so I guess I'll have to wait until I talked to daddy myself tonight.

"Alright, I will keep my mouth closed if you tell him today when he gets off and has had his dinner."

I couldn't believe she was really going to make me tell him. Two things I was sure of, one, I still don't know what to think about the dance or peter, and two, how was I going to tell my dad? I wasn't about to spend my Saturday trying to figure it out either, so I got dressed called down the street to

Tamika's house, my best friend to see if she is up.

"Hello Ms. Morgan is Tamika up?

"Tamika, Crystal's on the phone."

She informed Mika and I was placed on hold. While I waited, I heard Tamika and her sister going back and forth over the remote.

"Hey best friend."

"What are you doing now?"

"Nothing just put some clothes on."

"Good let's walk to the store?"

"Alright, give me five minutes."

"Okay bye."

Tamika is older than me, Tamika is taller than me, Tamika has a caramel skin complexion, she is already developed unlike; me a late bloomer, and she always wears her hair down. I figured I would talk to her about Peter. She had already had experiences with boys. I knew nothing about them other than how they look. Remembering one time when Mika was grounded and couldn't talk or go outside, I became her mouth piece for her boyfriend Tyrone. Tyrone would come to my house to leave her a message and I would deliver the message back to her. I asked my mom if I could walk to the store with Mika, she agreed and I was off. I met Mika on the sidewalk in front of her house. She hugs me.

"Hey girlfriend."

"Hey lady."

"So what are you getting from the store?"

"Actually, I wanted to talk to you about what happened at Pat's birthday party."

"Does it involve a guy?"

She caught me blushing, and her eyes lit up like a Christmas tree. How did she know? Looking down at the ground feeling shy.

"Sunshine, you better spit it out right now."

"Okay already Peter asked me to dance and we danced."

She was as shocked as I was and I was the one who danced. Jumping up and down clapping her hands pulling me close to her.

"How was it?"

"How was what? It was my first dance."

"Did you guys exchange numbers?"

"No I don't think he wanted my number Mika, just a dance."

Peter getting my number would never happen. My mom or my dad would not have a boy calling me unless they are family. Now I feel like I said too much which will make me relive that moment.

"Let me get this straight, you didn't get his number, but you two danced, okay now what?"

"Nothing he will stay on Clifford and I will stay on yak."

"I guess if you say so."

We finally made it to the store and I bought hot chips and juice and she bought a candy bar and a pop. On our way back home, there was this awkward silence between us almost all the way back to her house. I really didn't want to discuss Peter anymore, so I knew I had to change the subject, but I know she's still thinking about it and she was just waiting on me to bring it up.

"Mika, did you ask your mom if you can come to church with us in the morning?"

"Yea I did, she said no because I have to help her clean out her basement."

My mom always took us to church which was no problem to me at times however, sometimes I did wish I could stay at home. Most of the times I'd be ready and willing to go, because I get to be with my friends at church. I wanted to introduce Mika to my friends at the church. We sat on the porch and talked the day away like we usually do. It was time for me to have dinner. I almost forgot I had to have the talk with my daddy and I was not looking forward to that conversation. It made me very nervous, my stomach started to turn as I approached my house.

My mouth started to get dry and my throat is on fire. I had to pull myself together before I faced the man who was made of steel. I washed up and prepared myself for dinner and the conversation. Everybody is at the table and I am the missing link. We had a big table for an even bigger family. My mom gave birth to eight children; six girls and two boys.

The table was long and wooden we sat four to each side. Mom and dad sat at each end of the table. Cherish, Michael, myself and Brittany are on one side. On the other is Michelle, Tanisha, Shelly, Mitchell. From oldest to youngest, the order will be Cherish, Michael, myself, Brittany, Michelle, Tanisha, Shelly and Mitchell. The food smelled mouthwatering and we are ready to dig in. We had green beans, Cornbread, baked chicken and mash potatoes. After dad said grace, it is time to eat. Small conversation always took place at the table, but I am hoping and praying nobody brought up Peter.

After dinner, everybody scattered except me. I stayed to help mom clean up hoping she would give me some pointers about talking to daddy.

"Mom, I really don't know what to say to him."

"How about the truth?" She said with an outburst of laughter.

"Mom, I'm really scared over here and you're laughing at me."

"Baby I'm sorry, but you are really making something out of nothing."

"You think so?" I started to feel more relaxed after our conversation and maybe she was right.

"Thanks mom."

"Anytime Sunshine, now get in there while he is too full to move." She said laughing at me again but this time placing a kiss on my forehead.

Dad is in his den watching the sports channel. I really

didn't want to interrupt but I knew I had to or else. Here goes nothing.

"Hey Daddy."

"Hey Sunshine."

"How was your day at work today?"

He paused. Oh lord, I have his attention and he is staring at me with expectation. I felt like I was in court getting ready to testify about my own life. Never taking his eyes off me.

"It was work, so what's the meaning for this visit?"

"I kind of have to tell you something." The volume on the TV was muted and it was only his breathing that could be heard.

"Sunshine, enough of this, what is wrong?"

"Dad there is nothing wrong besides me having my first dance with a boy."

I finally said it with one eye open. I was glad he knew and it felt like a load was lifted off my shoulders.

"Oh really! Who is this boy? Do I know him or his parents?"

"Yes really, Peter Jackson and I don't believe you know his folks."

"The Jackson's boy? You know that boy is trouble? I don't think it will be a good idea for you to see him again.

"Well dad, it's not like we are dating it was only, I repeat only a dance."

"Okay you go get ready for bed." He told me while kissing me on the cheek.

"Goodnight daddy."

I left the lion's den glad to still be alive and in one piece as I honestly didn't know what to expect, but I'm glad it's over. Walking to my room noticing everybody was getting ready for bed. Cherish is hogging up the bathroom as usual and Michael is trying to get in there. That's something I can't understand, because our house has two full bathrooms and he will always fight over the one upstairs. Passing the twins' room, I heard mom reading Shelly and Mitchell a bedtime story. I remember those days, and my favorite book was the little mermaid. I showered, changed into my pajamas and grabbed my journal.

Dear Journal,
Today I was forced to tell my dad about the dance with Peter. It went good, I mean, he didn't go crazy on me. Well I'm glad it's over with and he knew. Between Tamika jumping to conclusions about Peter wanting my number and my dad warning me about Peter. I'm feeling really confused about him.

Sunday mornings are always the busiest, and it feels like a whirlwind goes through the house. After we have breakfast, the race is on. Everybody rushes to get dressed. Momma usually is the last one dressed. Once she is dressed we use both cars to drive to church. The smaller ones will ride with mom, because she has all the car seats. When at church I love to hear the music and sometimes it makes me want to sing. I know I will never sing in front of people, but I do sing to myself in the bathroom and my bedroom. I'll have my own concert in my room and entertain myself.

The church is very antique looking surrounded with bible quotes. What stood out the most to me inside the church there is a picture of a black Jesus. Everybody who came isn't black, so I guess they didn't mind. The way we sit at home is the way we sit at the church. Mom sat at one end and daddy sat at the other with all of us in the middle of them. Sometimes, services were held longer than others. Pastor Thomas brought the word today and when he was done he invited the people to come to Jesus. So many people got up and went to Jesus, and sometimes I wonder if I ever will go to Jesus. After church we have to sit down while our parents speak again and say their goodbyes. The longest process ever.

Finally, back at the house, clothes and shoes are tossed

everywhere and it's really a mess when everyone is done. This is the only day that Daddy helps mom with dinner. It's like their routine on Sundays. We eat a lot of chicken almost every other meal. One day, we all will grow feathers and be on the dinner table. After dinner, instead of helping I went straight upstairs to my room. Only to get called back downstairs to the phone.

"Hello."

"Hey cousin, what are you doing?" It was Pat and I was surprised.

I wonder what he was calling for.

"Hey cousin, nothing just finished eating dinner. What's up?"

He paused as if he was debating if he wanted to go on with our conversation.

"I actually have someone who wants to talk to you."

No way can this be happening? First the dance, Tamika telling me he wanted my number and my dad telling me he's trouble. Maybe I shouldn't talk to him. What if it's not even Peter who wants to talk to me?

"Who?" I asked, remaining as calm as possible.

"Hello"

The next voice I hear is not my cousin. This voice sent chills of electricity through me. Why is Peter having this effect on me and what is going on with me? Questioning myself.

"Hey Peter." What's up?

"You tell me?"

"There's not really much to tell." The mellow sound of his laughter relaxed me.

"Okay, how about you tell me what you did today?"

"I went to church with my family maybe you can come one Sunday?"

"Church, me? I don't know about that, if I walk through those doors we will all burn."

We both laughed uncontrollably.

"Well that will be a risk we all will have to take when you are ready."

"See, I'm laughing and I like the fact you are talking to me. We should do it more often?"

Tamika was right, he wants to keep talking to me, but I can't talk to boys, so it's not a good idea.

"Peter I... Don't know if that's a good idea. How old are you?"

"I'm the same age as you 15. Is my age a problem?"

No I was really looking for a reason to avoid the continuation of this conversation but failed horribly, because he is my age. Sure I'll just tell him my daddy thinks he's trouble and I can't talk to him, but then he will think I am a baby. Only fifteen, the same age as me. I'm running out of legit reasons. I needed to think of something and fast.

"Okay, maybe we can arrange that."

I finally said the opposite of what I was thinking, containing the firework display that was going off inside me.

"Really?" He sounded surprised.

"Peter I have to go."

I didn't want to bring unwanted attention to me or this phone especially since Michael walked by here twice.

"When can I talk to you again?" Honestly I had no idea, so I couldn't answer his question right now.

"Soon, bye."

He hung up and left me with a thousand questions. I guess I'll get my chance to interrogate him soon enough. The phone rang as I walked away.

"Hello."

"Yea put Eddie B on the phone." The voice is low and husky, it's Uncle Richard for dad.

"Hold on, Daddy telephone."

I yelled as loud as I could sitting the phone down making my way back to my room. I didn't want to be there when he came to the phone. When I was back in my room watching TV, I heard a knock on the door. It was already opened and I looked up to see Cherish standing there.

"Hey, can I come in?"

"Yea."

She comes in and sits with me on the bed and there's silence at first. Then she pushes me almost off the bed I grabbed the covers which kept me from falling off the bed, and I stared at her.

"That's for dancing with a boy before me and not talking to me about it."

"Well the night of the party you didn't say anything, so I didn't either." I shrugged my shoulders up.

"You're right, I was waiting on you, but it's going on a year and still nothing."

She was right, I hadn't said anything to her because I honestly thought she was not interested. She was really wrong it has not been a year. We both laughed.

"Cherry Berry I really thought you didn't care, or wanted to talk about it, sorry." Sounding and looking sad with my bottom lip poked out.

"No you put that lip away." She said playfully.

"Okay what is it that my biggest sister wants to know?"

Not sure if I was ready for this conversation. I mean, we never talked about boys before, so why now? I asked myself but I was up for it.

"Well I was told he smelled like a bag of onions, did he?"

The nerve of those witches Sarah and Nicole. With one eyebrow raised, I responded to her.

"You heard that also, well let me assure you Pete did not stink."

"Hold up! Did you just call him Pete?"

She was right Pete was out before I even realized it. I hope she doesn't think too much into it. He did call me Crissy, he never calls me Crystal or Sunshine, names that I'm actually familiar with.

"I did call him Pete."

She said nothing for a minute which felt like 60 minutes. Staring at me with her head cocked to the side. Looking at me, watching me, studying me. She finally said something.

"You really like him."

I laid back on the bed with my hands behind my head.

"I guess you are right."

"No, we are not guessing on this one, we know." She smiled.

"What are your plans for Peter?"

Plans? I had no plans and Peter is only thought of when I had to bring him up. I couldn't tell her what daddy said. She would just disagree. Sometimes I think she forgets she's the one who's 18 and I have a couple more years to go.

"I don't have any plans, this is my first time even looking at a boy differently, what can I do?"

"Yea about that." She pops up off the bed runs to the door and says.

"You can talk to your momma about that."

She was gone like the wind and disappeared in the shadows of the hallway. I thought about what we talked about. I did like Peter and what I couldn't figure out was whether me liking him is a good or bad thing? Tomorrow is school and we are preparing for our last dances of the year. Cherish is getting ready for prom and Michael and I are getting ready for the Grand Slam. The prom is for the seniors and the Grand Slam is for the tenth and the eleventh graders. I've been so busy dealing with feelings I've never had concerning Peter that I forgot about the dances.

Cherish is graduating, she had completed her last year at Bailey High. I wonder what she will be doing next? I wish it was me and it's funny how time flies. Speaking of time, I looked up and saw it is time to call it a night.

Dear Journal,

Tomorrow is school and I haven't really faced any other boys since Peter. What if Peter changed the way I viewed boys? I know Derrick is always extra nice to me. Derrick will carry my books to class and hold my book bag. I mean, Derrick is really a sweetheart when it comes to me. Peter and I didn't attend the same school, so at least it will be easier to face Derrick without feeling weird. I still needed a date for the dance and an outfit. P.S. too many things going on.

CHAPTER 2

Dad dropped everybody off at school the next morning. Shelly and Mitchell were the only ones not in school yet, however, when they turn of age, they will start school I'm sure. When dad goes to work he is the unstoppable Sheriff Hartland. Dad has been a sheriff since I could remember, so I figured he likes being the sheriff or the pay with benefits? He will drop off the younger ones first and then us. Pulling up at our school, the home of the Brave heart. Bailey High appeared to be a big school on the outside, however, if you asked me it felt smaller on the inside. I'm on my second year, but my first year was horrible. I had to wear glasses which made me a targeted freshman.

My year as a freshman was full of memories I'm not fond of. I wasn't a bad looking girl, yet a couple of pounds bigger than the next, also I had to wear glasses and I was taller than most girls. That's when I met Derrick Lester, he befriended me in the middle of all the chaos of being teased. The day he stood up for me was the day things started to change. Derrick was in a higher grade than me at the time, which made it even better. He came to my rescue right in the middle of a bullying session. Latonya and her band wagon had all their insults during lunch period. I guess he heard them and stepped up and took over. He put them in their place and they left with sour faces. I will always be grateful to him for his heroic action.

"Hey Crystal, good morning"

Derrick said meeting me at the entrance of the school.

"Hey you."

Do you have your presentation ready for your class?"

"I've been working on it, so I hope I'm prepared enough." We both laughed.

"You know I don't do public speaking it's not my cup of tea, just give me a court and a ball and I'll be the star in the room."

"Look at you so full of yourself."

Pushing him in the shoulders before he could respond, we were interrupted by the second school bell. Which meant it was the tardy bell.

"Saved by the bell." He said pushing me into class.

School was a drag as usual, and it was going by slowly. I looked up and it was time to go to lunch. I had pizza, veggies, and chocolate milk. I sat at the table with friends, and we talked about the upcoming dance. I see I wasn't the only one who hadn't picked out a dress for the dance, and time was slowly approaching. They started talking about bringing dates which made me twist my lips. Having a date was the last thing on my mind. It did make me think about Peter but I knew it wasn't going to happen, so dateless I will be that night. I must've been deep in thought, because I didn't realize the lunch room was clearing out.

"It's time to go," The lunch aide reminded me and I was up on my feet.

Throwing the trash away and placing the tray in the right place with two more classes to attend, gym and science. Science wasn't so bad my teacher Mr. Miller made science fun to learn, especially if he knew we were struggling with his class. The gym class was cool also. I mean a bunch of hormones running around freely, who couldn't resist that? I really enjoyed swimming, however, I hated that swimming class was closer towards the end of the day. In the winter, walking home was the worst. Thinking about it sent chills up my arms. The summer was more bearable. We didn't swim today because the pool was being cleaned. Not swimming today was actually a plus for me, because my hair was done and it was able to stay hanging down.

Finally, the day was over and it was time to go home. I went to the locker to get my jacket as it was springtime, so I still wore something small and comfortable. It wasn't too heavy and it wasn't too light, but just right for the season. Derrick met me at the locker ready to carry my book bag.

"Hey."

Derrick said while reaching for my book bag. Most people always thought I was using him, but in a way, I am, but he is my friend who wanted to carry my book bag and I allowed him to.

"Thank you." I said flashing my pearly whites.

"No problem."

We walked outside and the breeze was thick, the leaves on the trees started to grow back, and the sun was shining bright. My heart beat started to race, it felt like I was running a marathon without my feet, because my feet are froze and I am motionless; stiff as a statue. I hear other voices talking to me, but I only see Peter hugging Stacey. I mean, let me correct myself, pretty Stacey at least that's what the other boys calls her. Stacey was tall, skinny, light skinned and her skin looked smooth as silk, and her hair black and full. Sometimes she looked like she walked fresh off a magazine. I was trying to stop staring before he had noticed me, so I made it my business to get lost in the crowd.

"Crystal, are you okay?"

Derrick asked me and I heard the concern in his voice, but truth be told I wasn't sure if I was okay. I felt my ears burning and my face turning red. What was going on with me? Was I jealous?

"I don't know, come on let's go this way."

Leading Derrick in the opposite direction of Peter, Derrick looked confused, but he followed.

"Crissy"

I heard my name being called twice coming from behind me, however, I didn't stop I kept walking but even faster. Never looking back, but Peter was getting closer. Peter grabbed my hand and turned me around to face him. He was smiling and I wanted to smack that smile right off his face, but before Peter could say anything, Derrick made his presence known.

"I don't think she wants to be bothered."

Derrick was protective of me placing his body between Peter and I. Peter wasn't getting to me unless he went through Derrick.

"I don't want any problems."

Peter said throwing his hands up in a surrendering position laughing, but being serious and remaining stern in his stand. I'm praying to god please don't let these boys start fighting. Honestly, I couldn't handle it. Never taking his eyes off of me, Peter speaks.

"Crissy can talk for herself and if she wants me to leave, I will do exactly that."

Derrick looked at me trying to read me and see if there is any truth to what was just said. We locked eyes and I nodded my head to assure him it was okay. Derrick let out a regretful sigh and handed me my book bag. I saw something I've never seen in Derrick's eyes and in those dark black eyes was hurt and disappointment. My heart sunk in my chest, because I knew I was part of the reason he was hurting. I tried to comfort him by giving him a hug. The hug was different; it was colder than an ice cream cone on a summer day. He looked at me and walked away. I was speechless and I didn't know what to say. I just watched my friend walk away.

"See what you did?" Turning back to Peter.

Peter showed no concern for Derrick's feelings at all. He was actually still teasing him by waving his hand from side to side with a devilish smile on his face. Bringing his attention back to me, I pushed his shoulders.

"Okay Peter enough, what do you want?"

"Crystal, what's with the attitude?"

I can't believe he just asked me what my problem was as if he wasn't here and witnessing the same thing. I rolled my eyes, fixed my book bag, turned on my heels and started walking home.

"Wait up and slow down."

He said but I was heated and I couldn't stop. My feet wouldn't let me and I was a one-woman marching band. With my head over my shoulder looking back my hair hanging down so he couldn't see my face all the way and I yelled.

"Why don't you go walk with pretty Stacey?"

I couldn't believe those words came out of my mouth. Now he's going to know I saw him hugging her. The sounds of his shoes hitting the ground ceased.

"Crissy can you please stop and talk to me?"

As much as I wanted to keep walking. I stopped instantaneously. It was the seriousness in his voice that pierced my heart to the core. He ran a couple of feet towards me and now we are face to face. I felt the warmth of his body and the piercing of his brown eyes looking down at me, it was making me weak in the knees. I refused to let him see me sweat, so I placed my hands on my hips, stared him straight in the face, and broke the silence.

"What is it?"

With all the irritation in my voice, I hope he heard and felt all of it. After all, it was because of him I was irritated and experiencing feelings I've never felt.

"It's not what you think."

"So I just didn't see you hugging on pretty Stacey? Because that's exactly what I'm thinking."

"Girl can you stop it with this pretty crap."

Now he sounded irritated, throwing his head to the back. Maybe this is a good thing, and he knows how I'm feeling irritated with him.

"I would rather hug pretty Crystal."

He reached for my hands but I snatched them back. He was not getting off that easy. The bigger question is, why do I even care?

"You know what, you can hug whoever you want it is not my business."

"Crystal I'm sorry I hugged her, I'm sorry you saw it, and most of all, I'm sorry for upsetting you."

His face is full of regret. Can he be telling me the truth?

"You don't have to apologize, I'm not your girlfriend and maybe I'm over thinking a situation as usual. I should be asking for your forgiveness for putting my nose in your business."

"You're right about one thing."

The nerve of him to agree with me. I rolled my eyes even harder. He laughs.

"You are not my girlfriend, but what if I wanted you to be my girlfriend?"

Blushing, I turned my face from his gaze and looked at the ground. When looking down, my long black hair was hiding my face. Peter pulls my hair back on both sides, which brought my attention back to him. By all means, I was not about to agree to be his girlfriend. Looking past his smile, I heard my daddy's voice. *He's trouble.* What if my daddy didn't see what I saw in Peter? Trying to change the entire mood and situation, I took off my book bag and gave it to him.

"Here." Shoving it in his chest. He stumbled back and smiled.

"Come on."

Leading us in the direction of our homes, we walked and talked. It was never a quiet moment between us. He wanted to know about me and me him. I found out his family is smaller than mine and he has a fraternal twin. Haven't met him come to think about it, he wasn't even at the party. He knows my older sister and brother better than I thought. They all played together growing up. When Peter stopped walking, it made me look up at him puzzled with one eyebrow raised. He smiled and pointed, so I followed his finger. Embarrassment filled my face, because I was looking at my house.

"Oh, yea thanks." I said getting my book bag.

"Trust me, Crystal it was my pleasure."

"You don't have to walk me home every day."

"You're right, but if I want to I will."

Leaving before I could even respond. I didn't know where Peter and I were going and I'm not sure of Peter's motives, but I planned on finding out. Letting myself in, hoping no one saw Peter. Hanging my jacket up in the closet praying I was in the clear and my secret will be safe with me. Holding my breath feeling like a burglar in my own house walking through it. Dinner smelled delicious making my way in the kitchen to see what we were having. The worst part about going in the kitchen was that we had to pass our parent's room. With one foot on the kitchen floor.

"Sunshine."

There it was my mom's calm voice. I'm caught. Jumping and feeling me deflate like a helium balloon, I looked at her standing there with her arms crossed on her well-developed chest. I was over preparing myself for every punishment because of Peter. Bathroom duty for a week, dishes for a week, laundry for a week, grounded in my room for a week, or worse, a whooping and I didn't want either one of those punishments.

"Hey momma."

Running giving her a hug, I tried to keep my composure and show no other emotions but happiness to see her. Stepping back from her studying me carefully, her dark brown eyes pierced my insides.

"Where are your sisters and brother?"

"They all had to stay after school and I didn't feel like waiting."

"Why didn't you call me? You know I would've came and picked you up."

"I know mom, it's nice outside so I decided to walk with some friends who had to come the same way."

"Okay don't take your tail in my kitchen looking in my pots either."

Walking back in her room, I charged in the opposite direction towards the stairs because she was not going to get a rebuttal from me. In my room, I grabbed a magazine off my desk. Going through the magazine to see if I can get any ideas for a dress or a hairstyle. Cherish was using it and she left it on my desk when she was done. I figured it helped her so it could have done the same for me. Cherish' prom theme is One Night Only Michael and my theme is Enchantment under the Sea. Excited to wear a dress or a woman suit outfit my choice of required clothes. I needed to hurry up and make a choice quickly because time is of the essence and I didn't want to wait to the last minute. My stomach started to growl that was my cue to head to dinner. Closing the magazine feeling defeated because it wasn't useful at all. My search will have to continue.

Making my way downstairs to see everybody was at home. It didn't appear that I missed anything while upstairs. The aroma of soul food was in the air. I loved when my momma cooked. Actually, it is one of my highlights when I come home. During dinner, daddy told us he knew our dances are coming up and we still have a curfew. No surprise there of course, we weren't happy with it, but we understood the reasoning behind it.

"I'm 18, and I will be staying out all night. Catch me the next morning."

Cherish protested. Mom and dad paused and looked at each other. I was wondering who was going to say something first. I was trying to get the attention of Michael, but he had his face buried in his hands. This can't be good. I always thought her mouth will get all of us in trouble one day.

"Excuse me." The voice of mom was always serene.

"Come on mom, you and dad still treat me like a kid, so why can't I hang out with my friends?"

"Alright cherish, what will be a reasonable time for you?"

I didn't know which one is worse the fact that the question was asked, or my dad asked the question. I studied my dad trying to figure his intentions, but I was lost. He was eating and paying little attention to the answer of his own question. When mom and dad teamed up in front of us, it was never a good sign that the situation will go in our favor. Kicking Cherish' leg under the table hoping she would shut up. While staring at me shaking my head and moving my lips in slow motion saying no with no words coming out. She rolled her eyes and ignored me, of course, she finished what she started.

"Being the responsible senior that I am, I believe 2:00 a.m. is reasonable."

My mouth dropped to the table. I can't believe she actually said 2 in the morning. What's worse is that she said it with confidence!

"Okay, enough of this! Why can't you just come home at 12? You are not special, just older."

I guess Michael just had to add his two cents. Cherish just smacked her lips and gave him a look that said mind your own business.

"You hear that Eddie B? Our child wants to walk in our house at 2 in the morning."

"Yea, Fay I heard it."

Daddy said rubbing his chin staring at my momma. This can't be good and I wasn't interested in seeing the outcome.

"Can I be excused?"

I said standing up, plus I was full anyway and just wanted to get away from this conversation. Both parents stared at me before they answered.

"Sit down Sunshine."

Darn there was no getting out and away from this table. Sitting here watching everyone else eat while drinking my water, we are all patiently waiting for them to respond. They actually made us wait until they were done.

"If it's 2 o'clock you want, then 2 o'clock you will have."

Daddy said that calmer than the sea Jesus spoke to.

"Yes." Throwing her hands up in the air like she made a touchdown.

"One condition." Momma said pointing her finger at Cherish.

"That following week, you will be responsible for all the chores."

"But mom you know I can't do everybody chores. That's not fair."

"The choice is yours, so be sure to choose wisely, and now you may leave the table Sunshine."

Daddy finally excused me from the table and I disappeared like a David Copperfield magic trick. I didn't even want to know Cherish' choice and it sucked to be her now. I don't know why she can't just come home the regular time, nevertheless, I hope she don't mess it up for me. My sanctuary is calling my name. Falling back in my bed exhausted mentally from that beautiful performance Cherish displayed. For the most part, I didn't hear any yelling downstairs, so maybe everyone was happy with her choice.

Dear Journal,
School was school. My action didn't start until after school. Peter came up to the school and hugged pretty Stacey and that made me angry, he made Derrick mad and that hurt my feelings. He apologized and walked me home. I felt bad for Derrick and I couldn't call him, so I had to wait until I went back to school. What if he didn't speak to me at all?

Immediately pushing that thought out my head, closing my journal. There was a light tap on my door.

"Come in." to my surprise it is my Mika and I am happy to see her.

"Hey girlfriend."

"Hey, your momma freed you?"

"Yeah man only to your house though."

Mika stayed in trouble or on a punishment more than anyone I knew. She noticed the magazine on my bed and started to inquire.

"Any luck with finding ideas for your outfit?"

"Girl no, and I'm done looking in that ugly magazine."

"Just because it wasn't useful doesn't mean the magazine is ugly."

"Your point?" that's ok because when you are done pleading your case, the magazine still will be ugly." Waving my hand at her.

"What if we dressed alike?"

"No way, are you serious?"

"Serious as a heart attack."

"Okay."

"Alright we can have my mom take us to look for something to wear."

She saw me pulling away from the conversation, my facial expression always gives me away. I don't mind dressing alike, but her momma drove like a bat out of hell that scared me.

"What is it Sunshine?"

"Nothing for real, but you know how I feel about your momma driving."

We both laughed. Filling her in on the action today that included Peter. She seems to think Peter really likes me. If that was true, I don't know why he would? She tried to convince me I'm in denial.

"What about a date? You should ask Peter to the dance?"

"That's not going to happen. Wait, you have a date?"

"Duh."

"Who?" I guess I shouldn't be surprise she is good when it comes to the opposite sex.

"James Johnson." He asked me in third hour today.

"Sweet." Placing my hand in the air for a high five.

We talked more and then we played some music and did some dancing until we tired ourselves out. It was always fun hanging with Mika. Mika's phone started to vibrate, yes she has a cell phone. It is her mom letting her know it was time to come home. This is why she stays in trouble because even after the text message she didn't leave until ten minutes later. I had to put her out because I felt myself getting sleepy. I was glad my room is in the back of the hallway because when I slept I was less disturbed by the noise in the house. I went to sleep thinking about Peter. I still was in shock with the way Peter handled Derrick, and I had to admit maybe my dad was right just a little bit.

The next day of school it was weird. I didn't see Derrick until lunch and even then he didn't speak. If he was trying to make me hurt like he was hurt yesterday his plan is working. I couldn't understand why. I didn't even know Peter was coming, but today I knew there was a possibility Peter may be coming. Michael, Brittany and Cherish will see him today especially since they didn't have to stay after school. Before sitting down at the lunch table, I made it my business to get Derrick's attention. Derrick was in the line which made it easier.

"Hey you not speaking to me?" As I used my shoulder to push against his shoulder.

"Hey Crystal." He was nonchalant.

He kept carrying on like I wasn't trying to converse with him. I was blown away by the way he is blowing me off. I've never seen him act like this with anyone. Grabbing his forearm with one hand.

"Come on Derrick, let us not do this."

"Do what Crystal? We are in the lunchroom and I'm supposed to be getting my lunch."

That was it, I got the point. I was not going to beg him to talk to me so I can express how sorry I am for yesterday. This was all Peter's fault and thinking about it made me angry all over again. I turned to walk away and find me a table. Sitting by myself I couldn't stand knowing Derrick was mad and it was my fault. Brittany saw me sitting by myself and came over.

"Hey sis why you over here sitting by yourself?"

"You wouldn't understand." Followed by a 12-inch-long sigh.

She placed her hand on my shoulder and said with such sincerity.

"I know I'm younger, but you will be surprised. Now my question for you is what boy has you over here moping alone?"

Staring at her with fascination, how could she read me like I was an open book? Am I really moping? Placing my head on the concave table with no desire to eat. Brittany walked away. While my head was on the table I felt a tap on my head. Looking up, it was Derrick. He was smirking, so I guess this was a good sign.

"Can I sit down?"

Without saying anything forcing myself to move over, because I can be stubborn at times and the nerve of him to come and talk to me when he was ready.

"It's a free country." I placed my head back on the table.

"Crystal look at me I didn't come over here to talk to the back of your head."

To be mad at me he sure is being demanding, but to avoid any more problems between us I complied with his request.

"Okay fine, is this better for you?" Readjusting myself to face him.

"Yesterday I was heated and it's because of your new boyfriend."

"First of all, his name his Peter and he is not my boyfriend."

"Good, so you are not taking him to the last dance?"

Giving me a wicked smile. He's worried about Peter and me going to the dance together. I've never been on a date let alone having a date for the dance.

"No, Peter is not coming to the dance with me."

"Will you go to the dance with me Crystal?"

The entire day he hadn't spoke to me and now he is asking me to the dance. I'm not sure if I should answer or if I want to go with him. Telling him no will make him mad all over again at me. On the other hand, telling him yes means Derrick will be my first date.

"Alright sounds okay to me."

"Really?"

He was surprised and excited about my answer. I can tell Mika I have a date also. Maybe we all can get picked up from my house.

"Derrick there is something you should know."

He tensed up like he was preparing for the worst in his mind.

"What's that?"

"Peter may be walking me home again."

Strangely he laughs, now I'm the one surprised.

"Okay no problem."

They are the last words Derrick said to me until after school. Derrick met me at my locker today like nothing ever happened. We are back to our regular schedule routine. We met everybody else outside. Peter and Michael are talking while Brittany and Cherish are standing on the side of them. Derrick and I walked up and all eyes are on us. Peter stared at me without blinking. Peter's stare placed me on an emotional roller coaster ride mentally and I wasn't coming off anytime soon. Finally, Michael spoke and broke the silence.

"Good, everybody's here lets' get this journey started."

We all started walking. Placing my hands inside of Cherish and Brittany, lord knew I needed some kind of comfort and support. While we walked behind the boys, Cherish whispered in my ear to ask if I was okay. I couldn't answer her because I wasn't even sure. Derrick brings up the dance to Michael and I was sure I did not like the direction this conversation was going in.

"Michael who are you taking to the dance?" Derrick asked.

"I'm not sure, however, I am thinking about asking Judy."

"No." Derrick shouted loudly.

Judy is a high maintenance female and Michael was so plain there's no way she will agree to go with him.

"What about you?"

There it is the question I was dreading to hear and the answer also. My feet stopped with no help from my brain because my brain was yelling run, but I couldn't move.

"I'm taking crystal."

I couldn't say anything seeing how he is telling the truth, however, I wish I could have made it known on my own terms. Feeling my face start to heat, I felt like I was going to pass out. If Cherish hadn't been a wall for me, the ground is where I would have been. Peter looked back at me and muttered.

"Oh really?" Everything about his reaction was if he was amused.

"Yea he asked today and I agreed."

Cherish, Brittany and Michael was shocked just as I was even being asked to the dance. It was too late to take it back, so I had to suck it up and prepare for the best first date. On the rest of the way home they talked sports and cars. The weather appeared to be changing for the better. The breeze was warmer than it had been. Traffic was heavier on the main streets.

When we made it home, everybody went their separate ways. Peter didn't even acknowledge me or my presence. I guess so much for him liking me. I already knew this will be a topic at the dinner table. I was bracing myself for the impact. Grabbing a banana off the table and did my homework. I helped Brit Brat with hers and when I was done, I took a clean sheet piece of paper out and started to doodle on it. I found myself writing Peter's name at least three times before I realized I was doing it. I put my things away and got ready for dinner. The best part about dinner is that daddy wasn't going to be at home for the open discussion however, I knew he still was going to find out.

While in my room reflecting on recent events, Peter's reaction to me going to the dance with Derrick was creepy. If he wasn't happy about it he sure didn't show it. Another thing is if he likes me like Mika says he does, how can he be okay with it? I really have to talk to Mika, these boys are making my head spin like a bottle top.

I was glad to see when I arrived down stairs the phone was open. I rushed and dialed her number before anyone called.

"Hey can I speak to Mika?"

Her brother answered the phone. She had two brothers and one sister. They all were close in their own way. Mika's older brothers didn't stay in the house they are grown, however, they will visit as much as possible. The background was quite I wonder where Trisha is, who her younger sister is.

"Hey Sunshine, What's going on?"

"Girl what's not going on? I need you sitting down for this."

She burst out laughing like I just told the joke of a lifetime.

"Why are you laughing at me?"

"Because you are special and you're always making a big deal out of everything."

"I have your big deal, so you're not the only one with a date for the dance."

"No." She screamed in laughter.

Talking about boys always seemed to excite her, honestly I couldn't figure out why though.

"Yes, Derrick asked me at lunch today."

"But I thought he was mad at you?"

"Well it's an even longer story, but what's crazy is that he made the announcement in front of everybody and that's including Peter. I was so lost I couldn't even register a single stable emotion. She starts screaming and laughing.

"What did Peter say? Or should I ask, what did Peter do?"

"That's the thing Mika he barely reacted at all."

"That's not good."

"What? What's not good?"

"Peter is either pissed at you or just doesn't like you anymore. I can't wait until I'm able to walk home again. I'm missing all the action."

Peter being pissed at me is understandable, but he not liking me any more sent a pain through my stomach and I cradled it like a newborn.

"Hold on Mika, my lines beeping."

"Okay."

"Hello Hartland residence." I attempted to disguise my voice.

"Yes are the parents of Crystal Hartland home?"

The other voice on the phone was unrecognizable. Whoever he was sounded very professional and what's worse, he knows my name asking for my parents.

"Yes who's calling?" I tried to hide the concern in my voice as much as possible.

"My name is Peter Jackson and I was calling to find out why Crissy agreed to go to the dance with some scrub?"

Relieved that it is Peter, however, I wasn't so sure about his question.

"Peter why are you playing on my phone? Wait a minute hold on." I clicked back on the other line.

"Hello Mika its Peter, so I'll just see you tomorrow."

CHAPTER 3

"Yea I'm back."

"Were you on the phone with him?"

"His name is Derrick and nope."

"But you are going to the dance with him?"

"Yep those are my plans."

"Okay let me get this straight, so I tell you that I want you as my girlfriend and you're going out with another guy?"

He's right, he did tell me he wanted me as his girlfriend, but I never agreed. Trying not to say anything else to avoid a potential argument, I gave the cat my tongue.

"Uh hello Crystal, don't get quiet on me now."

"I don't know what you expect me to say Peter."

"How about why the lame Derrick is taking you to the dance?"

I don't know who Peter thinks he is but being a teenager requires me to make my own choices and choosing to go to the dance with Derrick is final. There's no taking it back now and risk hurting Derrick all over again.

"Look Pete, I understand this may cause you to feel a certain way, but after our first walk home I feel like I owe Derrick that much."

"So I'm Pete now?"

"No you are still Peter."

"But that's not what you just called me."

Peter was right and as much as I hate being wrong, I was not going to win this debate.

"Okay, are we going to argue about your name? Because if so, I have other things that require my attention!"

"Listen to you miss attitude, anyway go ahead to the dance with that kid and I want you to enjoy yourself."

He can't be serious? Peter and his nonchalant attitude is starting to get on my nerves. I wanted to scream all kinds of sailor words at him, but I didn't managing to keep cool.

"First of all, you are giving me your permission like I asked for it or I need it. The last time I checked, I've already agreed."

He just laughed, but why is he finding me amusing? I'm honestly ready to explode because of his calm stance. How does he hold his emotions together so well? Saved by my name that was being called in the background in which he heard also I couldn't get my next thoughts out; he beat me to it.

"Let me guess. you have to go?"

"Yes I do. Now if you'll excuse me and my attitude."

"Alright Crissy I'll get at you later, and oh yea, don't forget to have fun with Derrick."

Ugh the nerve of him slamming the phone on the couch. My name was called a second time, let me go before they send the rescue party.

"Hey daddy."

Inside the lion's den he was waiting for me. The wrinkle in his eyebrows was an indication he knew about my date. Taking a deep breath in and releasing slowly.

"I hear you have a date for the dance." Even though he knew it, it is still hard to verbalize it with my dad. Shaking my head up and down agreeing with him.

"Who is he?"

Pausing because his look became intense, his whole persona changed. Then my light bulb came on; he thinks it's with Peter. This is perfect they tell him I have a date, but failed to tell him who my date is.

"Dad, relax it's not with who you think. His name is Derrick Lester."

"Franny and Frankie's Kid."

"Yep that's him."

"Okay you kids have fun and no touching."

Just like that, it was over and it went better than expected. It was enough of this long emotional day. It was time to wash all the mess away. Running the water nice and hot just like I love it, and I always make the bathroom steamy. While the water was filling up, I got my pajamas ready. After getting in the tub I had to adjust the hot water to make it bearable with cold water. When I left the bathroom, the aroma of aloe was lingering in the air. I felt so much better and relaxed.

Dear Journal,

Today was a confusing day. Between Derrick's announcement of us going to the dance and Peter showing no concern. I needed to sit on a couch and let it out. Where would I even begin? What will I do with this Peter character? He makes me have feelings I never knew I had. If only he was simple as putting my hair in a ponytail, but even then I have my struggles, but I manage.

Turning my music on listening for a while, I eventually drift off to dreamland.

Time was going by way too fast, Mika and I haven't found a dress yet. Peter hasn't called me again and he hasn't come back up to the school. I started to worry but I know he is okay because if he wasn't, I'm pretty sure Pat would have made it known when I saw him at church. Today dad and mom is taking us out skating. I really don't like skating, but it's a chance to bond with my whole family. We went to Bay Land Skating Ring. The music is hype, the floor is jam packed, and the crowd is energetic. Loving the lights at the skating ring they are like a flashing rainbow. Cherish and I became thirsty, so we decide to make a stop at the concession stand. The menu had all our favorite drinks. Fruit punch, strawberry lemonade, pop and the list can go on.

"Hey kiddos what can I get you?"

The middle-aged woman asked us from behind the counter. She always has an inviting smile when we come skating. I bought my favorite strawberry lemonade and Cherish bought a fruit punch. Sitting down on the stools enjoying our refreshing drinks, we are interrupted by pretty Stacey and Diamond. Girls envied them and boys wanted to date them. Stacey was a run way model in her on rights and Diamond was well developed in all the female places. Diamond has hips, thighs, breasts and a small waist. They weren't your typical mean girls, but they weren't the nicest ones either. Did they have to sit right next to us?

"Hey ladies. What's up? Are you all ready for the dances?"

I couldn't believe she is actually trying to make small talk with us. The whole scene was interesting. I just waved but Cherish spoke verbally.

"Do you ladies have dates?"

Okay I'm starting to become annoyed now, but I have to keep my composure. Why is she asking us about dates? Girl go get your life. Why are you here talking to us?

"I actually do, Derrick will be my date for the night."

"Really?" She sounded really relieved more than surprised

"What about dresses?"

"Nope."

Cherish finally chimed in as I was starting to feel I was in the conversation alone.

"We are still looking."

"Alright ladies nice talking to you but, we're heading back to the ring later."

Cherish and I stared at each other shrugging our shoulders and continued to drink our beverages. I couldn't believe Diamond didn't say anything, but never stopped staring like she was reading a book that captured her attention. Whatever, enough thinking about Stacey and Diamond. After a quick trip to the ladies room, we joined the family and it was on and popping. It feels so good to have all of us here, the twins were too young to skate, so they chilled in their stroller. After skating, we went to Captain Pizzeria for dinner. Captain Pizzeria is the spot to be for fun and family, they had people dressed up as pirates, and pirates doing karaoke to children's songs it is just entertaining. We ordered three pizzas, two pepperoni and one cheese pizza. Since we had plenty of juices and pop at the Bay Ring we only ordered water with our pizza. On the way home, I called shotgun so I sat in the front. The drive home was peaceful; we listened to some old school gospel music and relaxed.

Dear Journal,
Today was a fun family day. Spending time with the family we played, we ate, and we laughed. At the skating ring I saw Stacey and Diamond and Stacey tried to have small talk with us. Something that I'm still questioning is why she felt the need to say anything to us? Oh well, I may never know that answer.

The next morning me, Mika, Trisha, Brittany, Stacey and Michael all walked to school. It is always fun with them and we made Michael look really good being seen with Bay City's finest females. Crystal and I discussed the arrangements for us going dress shopping. I'm really not excited about her mom driving, but I'll suck it up and take one for the team.

Finally, arriving at school Derrick was waiting for me at my locker like usual, but he had a smile on his face like his mouth was being stretched from left to right. He started to look very suspicious which made me wonder what he is up to?

"Hey Derrick, what's going on?" Asking him trying to stay calm as possible.

"Nothing waiting on you." Shrugging his shoulders up.

Staring at him for a minute feeling confused, did he just flirt with me? No maybe it's all in my big head. When opening my locker, an envelope fell to the ground. Quickly Derrick kneeled to the ground to retrieve the envelope placing it in my hand. It was a blue envelope, my favorite color and it had Crystal on it.

"Open it" He says anxiously.

I don't know what's inside and I'm pretty sure I may not want to know. Opening the mail starting to read it, I couldn't believe my eyes. Derrick is pouring out his heart in this letter, and ending it with asking if I will be his girlfriend.

"Derrick, I don't know what to say?"

"Well you don't have to answer now, let's get you to class."

Derrick's smile was gone and I couldn't help but feel it was my fault. My brain is on a roller coaster ride. What was he thinking? We've been friends all this time and now he wants more than a friendship. The school bell interrupted my thoughts and I got off the coaster.

"Alright Crystal I'll see you at lunch."

"Sure okay."

Derrick was gone and I couldn't even think. Trying to get control of my thoughts especially having to face Derrick and these classes. I said a prayer and kept it moving. Time went by swiftly and it is lunch time. Making it my business to dodge Derrick like dodging a ball in dodge ball. Knowing the inevitable will happen which will be facing him in the lunch room. I wasn't ready to see him or answer his question.

Walking in the lunch room, everything was magnified from the voices, the smells, and the people. The first person to greet me is Brittany.

"Hey big sis"

Locking her arm up with mine and started to walk me to the lunch counter. Brittany was rambling and my mind is in another world. Brittany must have seen I wasn't here shaking my arm.

"Sunshine, where are you?"

"Am I that obvious?"

"Yes girl you put that apple off and on your plate 3 times now, what's really going on?"

Why does she always read me like a book? I'm the older sister it's supposed to be the other way around. She should be coming to me with her boy problems. Before I could speak.

"And don't give me that I won't understand speech."

Pointing her finger in my chest she made it hard for me to resist her. Giving into her demand, I sighed. "Derrick asked me to be his girlfriend today."

She was shocked as I was covering her mouth and shaking her head from left to right in slow motion.

After standing like a statue, she broke her silence.

"Well what did you tell him?"

"I told him nothing because I really don't know what to say. I mean Derrick is cute, Derrick is funny and Derrick is smart but…"

"He's not Peter." My mouth dropped, how did she know what I was thinking?

"You are right Brit, he is not Peter, but what does Peter have to do with anything?"

"Come on Sunshine we both know you like Peter it's no secret. Poor Derrick."

She muttered shaking her head. Great now she's staring off in space eating her lunch. What will I tell Derrick? I can't be your girlfriend because Peter already asked me, but no I can't tell him that. Shaking that thought off like a wet dog shaking off water.

"Earth to Brittany." Waving my hand in front of her face.

"I don't know what to tell you about this mess, poor Derrick."

"Why do you keep saying poor Derrick?

"That question should be last on your list. The question you should be concentrating on is will you be Derrick's girlfriend, because here he comes."

She jumped up and was gone like a spring breeze on a winters day. I can't believe she just left me hanging. Looking up to see Derrick taking his time walking towards me, he was looking happy. I just hope when we are done talking he still remains happy.

"Hey Crystal"

"Hey Derrick"

"Can I sit and join you?"

"Sure why not."

There is an awkward silence between us for the first time both of us are speechless. Placing his elbows on the table pulling his hands together.

"So have you thought about being my girlfriend?"

Wow straight to the point.

"Yes I have."

"And what you say?"

"Look Derrick you are a great guy, a great friend and I know you will make a great boyfriend, but just not for me. "

"Okay I respect that." He said shaking his head up and down.

That's it; okay just like that this conversation is done? I couldn't read his emotions, so I had to ask.

"Does this mean you don't want to still be my date for the dance?"

"Crystal you are my friend and always have been and if you never be my girlfriend I can be happy with you as my friend."

He was so cool with my answer it was actually unexpected. The bell rung and it was time to go our separate ways. Wondering if he's going to walk me to class. Derrick did spoil me with his acts of kindness.

"Come on let's get you to class."

He stands up offering me his hand with a boyish grin flashing his perfectly shaped teeth. How can I say no? Placing my hand in his and we are off to class. I have to admit things felt like they were back to normal between

Derrick and I which made me feel better the rest of the day. Before I went to my last class I made a pit stop to the ladies room. I had to make sure it was empty before I started peeing. My pee is shy in front of strangers. Right when I was done, I heard the door open and voices full of giggles and laughter filled the atmosphere. Preparing myself to leave the stall.

Stepping out and that's when I see Stacey and Diamond. Nodding my head they paused smiled and continued talking. While soaping my hands up trying to make this uncomfortable situation move a little bit faster. I froze like a freeze pop when Stacey started talking about Peter. How cute he is and how she wonders if he had a girlfriend. I tried my best to ignore them, but I couldn't. The very thought of her talking about him like that made me angry.

"Who Peter Jackson?" Asking them apparently starling both of the girls.

"Yea that's him." Stacey stared at me intensely. "Well does he have a girlfriend?"

"He actually does." Her smiled quickly turned into a frown.

As for me, I was doing a victory dance in my head for scoring a touchdown. Diamond saw the disappointment on her friend's face. Diamond shot me a look if looks can kill I would be dead.

"Come on Stacey don't sweat it, how do you know if she is telling the truth?"

"You're right D she could be lying to us."

Perfect now she is giving me as if looks could kill look. I had to think of something fast.

"Well you both do know Peter is my cousin's best friend? I have had my share of hearing their conversations about girls and I never heard him mention Stacey, but some girl her name starts with a C I can't remember what it was now.

"Alright Stacey enough of this."

Diamond says grabbing her friend's hand heading for the door. They left me alone and staring at my reflection in the mirror. Laughing at the girl in the mirror I can't believe I just did that. When I was done drying my hands I was on my to swim class. Today we all get to come out of the shallow side of the pool and attempt to tread water in the deep. I must say, everyone else was not ready to go over to the other side, but as for me I am excited and couldn't wait. Ms. Jones is a good teacher and if you failed her class it wasn't because of her teaching technique, but your ability to comprehend. Ms. Jones was preparing me for an upcoming swim meet. After school, we had made plans to walk to the park before we went home.

I was the last one to meet up outside after washing the chlorine out my hair I wanted to make sure I dried it real good. All eyes were on me because of my enormous afro. I couldn't resist it was a perfect day to let my hair be free out of the normal ponytail. Mika really didn't like the idea of my hair being freed she was always put together even on her down days, but wait I don't even know when that is. The whole crew was at the park Mika, Michael, Brittany, Derrick, a couple of friends from school, and Cherish even tagged along. I think she had her own intentions. She thinks I didn't know that her date for the prom stayed across the street from the park.

We played tag, hide and seek, and we used the playground equipment also for enjoyment. Dinner time was approaching so it was time to head home. Looking from the corner of my eye I saw Cherish and the guy sitting and talking on a bench. Michael placed his two fingers in his mouth and whistled which got everybody's attention. We all froze in place.

"Come on it's time to go."

Michael yelled out I hated when he told me what to do. He half listened to mom and dad himself, so why did he expect me to listen to him? But knowing how upset mom will be if we are late, I complied. Cherish took her precious time saying her goodbyes to the mystery guy. I guess it's time for me to ask her some questions, so I can know more or something about this guy. We used Mika's phone to let our parents know we are on the way home. A block away from the house we decide to race the rest of the way. I shouted out the demands. On your mark, get ready, set go and we were off. We all made it to the porch Brittany was first and Cherish was last. Everybody went in and I stayed out waiting on Mika to catch her breath before I walked her halfway down the street.

"You ready?" I asked.

"Yep let's go."

"Derrick asked me to be his girlfriend today!"

I was waiting for a grand respond, but she was cool calm and collective.

"Oh my goodness what did you say?"

"I told him I liked being his friend and he agreed he liked me being his friend, so we're still friends."

Stopping abruptly grabbing me by my arms.

"That's it, no fall out because you clearly told him no, right?"

"Of course I did, I wasn't expecting that reaction either, but it is what it is and we decided to stay friends and move on.

"Alright if you say so, see you tomorrow dress shopping time and don't worry the drive will be okay."

Man she was so excited, me on the other hand, I hated shopping and to make things worse her Momma was driving which was no motivation. Back at the house everybody was at the table, even daddy. Brittany and Michael are setting up the table. I washed my hands in the downstairs bathroom and joined the family. We had tacos and salad with no desert. My parents are really picky about what we eat and drink, so we drink a lot of water mostly with every meal. Since dad had a health scare, we eat and drink differently. I mean it took us some time to adjust, but we are good now.

"Sunshine you ready for tomorrow?"

"What's tomorrow?" Mom looked at me puzzled with one eyebrow raised.

"Oh yeah, yes and no."

"Now what kind of answer is that?"

"She's scared of Tamika momma driving."

Michael blurted out and everyone who understood what was said sent laughter throughout the house. I couldn't help but to laugh also.

"Sunshine, if it bothers you that much why didn't you say something? I spoke with Ms. Morgan earlier today while she was walking her dog and of course our girls became topic of discussion. We decided to meet up at Lightly Fashion."

Lightly Fashion is the coolest spot in Bay City for fashion. I am actually surprised that's where we are going.

"So you can ride with your momma and sister."

When daddy spoke, that settled it no debating his decision. Dinner was good and we were content. Helping my mom clean up and get the twins ready for bed. I even read a bedtime story, while she sat in the recliner chair in their room and rested her feet. When I was done, mom had already fell asleep, so I got her a blanket out the lining closet covered her up kissed her forehead and didn't wake her. Before I went in my room I checked on Tanisha and Michelle and they were putting on their pajamas.

"You girls okay in here?"

"Yes." They said together.

"Sunshine where is momma?" Tanisha asked in the cutest kid baby voice.

"Well momma fell asleep in the big chair."

"Awe man, but who is going to read us a story now?" Michelle asked with a sad face.

"I'll read it for you if you want me to."

"You know how to read too? Tanisha says.

"Yes I know how to read too." Pushing her nose in with my finger.

They lit up like a Christmas tree and both went to get me a book. What did I get myself into? They climbed in their bunk bed, Tanisha on top and Michelle at the bottom. By the time I got to the second book they were sound asleep. They slept with a night light, so before I left I made sure it was on. Leaving the room I ran into Brittany.

"Girl you just getting upstairs?" all this time I thought you were in your room.

"Nope I helped momma clean up and get the twins ready for bed because daddy was called back to work, but he'll be back in a couple of hours."

"Oh well I'm about to call it a night, goodnight love you."

"Love you too."

Peeking in Michael's room he was occupied with his game and Cherish was in her own world watching music videos. A desire to disturb her came over me, so I can ask her about her date; however I'm not sure if I really wanted to. I passed up the opportunity and went to my room sitting on the edge of my bed reaching for my journal.

Dear Journal,
Today was a good day and playing at the park was fun. I still haven't heard from Peter. I know maybe I'll have my mom take me to her sister's house so I can find out what's going on with him. I really hope we find a dress for all of us when we go shopping tomorrow.

The room is decorated beautifully, and the different shades of blue and green gave it an underwater fill. Everybody is dressed for the occasion. Where is my date? Why is Stacey staring at me? Starting to pay attention to the music that was playing and it is the same song from Pat's party. *'Found a tender roni and the roni is so right. I think I'm going to love her for the rest of my life.'* Next thing I see is Peter's hand being extended in my direction.

"May I?"

I knew he was asking me to dance again, but how? He didn't attend my school. Why was he here? Derrick was nowhere in sight so I accepted and we danced.

"You know I like you Crissy, so you need to stop playing and be my girlfriend."

Peter's words sent a warm sensation through my body if he wasn't holding me, I probably would have fell to the ground, but instead I fell in the sweet embrace and warmth of his arms. With my head on his chest we twirled around a few times and then he dipped me, we stared into each other eyes. I saw past the whole bad boy imagine he displayed for everyone to see. Lifting me back up placing his hand on my face holding it there, he brings his face closer to mine and I could smell the mint on his breath and feel the warmth of his mouth as he spoke.

"Can I kiss you?"

Opening my mouth to speak, but no words came out, so I just nodded my head in agreement with his request. Before he placed his lips on mine, the school alarm went off and everybody scattered even Peter. I jumped up calling his name realizing it was a dream which got the attention of Cherish, she came running in my room.

"Sunshine are you okay?"

"Yea I think so." Sitting up, I turned off my alarm clock.

"Some dream you were having, you care to share? I mean I know Peter was in it, but my question is what was he doing?"

Swinging myself over to the edge of the bed with both hands firmly pressed on each side and my feet dangling. I looked up at her and gave my most mischievous smile and said.

"Wouldn't you like to know?"

"Alright keep your stinking dream to yourself." She said while pushing my head playfully to the side.

"And you better hurry up before you get left."

Now I didn't care about getting left, I didn't like shopping anyway; however the thought of riding with Ms. Morgan scared me. Jumping up grabbing my lace short sleeve blue button up, my light blue jeans, my white chucks with the light blue soles running passed Cherish to the bathroom. Looking in the mirror and had a memory of Peter asking me for a kiss. The thought of Peter kissing me made my stomach feel a strange way, so I shook that thought out of my head and focused on finding a dress.

Arriving downstairs everyone was having breakfast, so I joined in.

"Sunshine Ms. Morgan called this morning and asked if Tamika can ride with us today?" She said she was called into work, so of course I told her that will be fine. Finish eating so we can go."

My day is starting off to a pretty good start. No riding with Ms. Morgan and Mika is riding with us. I just hope we find what we will be looking for.

"Mom I forgot to tell you that Mika and I decided to dress alike."

Before she could respond, big mouth Michael just had to say something.

"The double mint twins are going to the dance." Laughing hard at his own joke, typical Michael.

"Well Sunshine I think that's a great idea and you girls are going to look beautiful."

"Thanks momma" I said while sticking my tongue out at Michael.

The door Bell rung, Dad answers the door while we stayed at the table but we knew it was Mika. There she was with her Carmel smooth skin, pretty white teeth and her hair in a ponytail, which is something we don't see regularly. She said hello to everyone and Daddy told her she can have a seat until it's time to go.

"Alright big man, you're in charge while I'm gone please keep my house in order. Mom said to Dad while giving him a kiss.

"Not in front of company." Michael yells out.

We all laughed and walked out the house to the car. We took dad's car, but before we got in the car, I asked Mom for her keys to her van so I can go get some music for this drive. Mom and dad have two different tastes in music. Daddy likes Canton Spirituals and Momma likes Kirk Franklin, so I think I'm taking my mom's side on this one. I sat in the back with Mika, but before I got back there I popped a different cd in the radio. Mika and I passed notes the entire time when we talked about the conversation we didn't want them in the front to hear. I started a conversation first.

"Momma do you know who Cherish' date is?

Cherish threw me a look from the front seat like I can't believe she just asked that, so I just hunched my shoulders up and asked what? My question didn't bother my mom because she just busted out laughing like I said a joke.

"Yes Sunshine I know Cherish' date."

"Okay who is he?"

"Maybe she will tell you when she gets ready Sunshine."

"What's the big deal? You know who my date is."

"I don't want everybody in my business yet, no offense Mika."

She wasn't keeping it from me, but wasn't ready to talk in front of Mika, so it wasn't a big deal. I was over thinking something again. Mika wasn't even paying us attention she had her face in her phone. Man I'll be glad when I'm able to get a phone. I should put it on my birthday list, but who am I kidding Cherish or Michael didn't even have one and they are older than me. On a freeway sign I read Lightly Fashion next exit. I started to feel anxious and didn't know why. I was only shopping for a dress. It still made me anxious. I just hope we all find something. I can honestly say I was ready to get this over with.

Stepping out the car inhaling a deep breath, the smell of summer was in the air. Looking around and noticed this little place is crowed. Well here goes nothing.

CHAPTER 4

PETER

Waiting for my mom to get home from work is nerve wrecking. Being alone left me with plenty of time to think about recent events. Like expressing to Crissy how I wanted her to be my girlfriend and she acted as if I didn't. She didn't say no, but what's her problem? What's wrong with me? Am I her type? Maybe she knew about my daddy? Who am I kidding, everybody knew underground Peter Jackson and it doesn't help I am his name sake. The thought alone made me angry, yes I'm his name sake, but I am not my father and nor do I want to follow in his footsteps. My name being called by my momma brought me out of my thoughts.

"I'm in the kitchen." I yelled to her.

"Hey handsome" she said giving me a bear hug.

"How was your day? Oh tell me more about this girl. Who has my baby's attention?" Joining me at the table after washing her hands.

"Mom she is beautiful, sweet, smart and stubborn. I told her I wanted her to be my girlfriend and she said nothing."

"No!" she said laughing.

"Mom I'm serious I don't know what else to do?"

"I'm sorry baby, but it looks and sounds like you said and did enough. Give it time maybe she will come around."

"But what if she doesn't?

"Then she will miss out on a handsome, a respectful, and a smart young man. Baby whatever you cooked for dinner smells delicious."

"You mean what you cooked?"

She looked in the pots and saw the leftovers from yesterday that was warmed up. We shared a laugh and even though we laughed a lot, sometimes the sadness in her eyes from missing daddy is noticeable. Honestly I miss him also, but I couldn't bring myself to go visit him as often as I should. The sight of him being in prison is unbearable. When I left him every time I wanted him to come back with us, but him coming home wasn't my reality, so I took a break from visiting him. To people he was a criminal, but to us he is a father, a husband, a provider and a protector. The worst part sometimes is hearing the horrible things people say about him and how I look just like him.

"Baby is there something else on your mind?"

"What if she doesn't like me because of daddy?"

Trying to sound less hurt than I really am, but she is my momma and she knew me almost as good as me. Reaching over the table placing her hand on mine.

"Baby you look at me you are not him or his bad choices. You hear me and I don't care what these people think or say. Do you understand me?"

Nodding my head in agreement, because she is right.

"Now let's finish eating before our food gets cold."

The rest of dinner time we are quite. My mom looked like she was in deep thought, and I dared not to disturb her. I ate my food and stayed in my lane. When dinner was over I went to my room and played some video games. Playing video games was my past time and chilling with Pat. Hearing my mom calling my name informing me someone was on the telephone, so I had to go see who was on the line. A piece of me wanted it to be Crystal, especially since I haven't called her or seen her, but in the back of my head knowing it wasn't wishful thinking I guess.

"Hello."

"Hey Peter, it's Stacey."

Wow, now why is Stacey calling me? Better yet, how did she get my number? We're cool and all, but we never exchanged numbers. Oh well, she has it now might as well hear her out.

"Peter I know you're probably wondering how I got your number, but that's not important right now."

"Ok so what's so important that you get my number from God knows where and call me. What's going on girl?" I ask keeping my cool and trying to stay as calm and comical as possible.

"Well you know our dance is coming up and I was wondering if you will be my date?"

What? No way. She cannot be serious? The invite is flattering, but I can't go to the dance with this girl. One, I would rather go with Crystal, but she didn't ask me. Two, Stacey is cute, but I like Crystal and how will Crystal feel if she sees me there with her? Thinking about how she reacted when she saw me hugging Stacey. This can't end well if I go, but why do I care so much of what Crystal thinks? She won't be my girlfriend anyway.

"UH I don't know Stacey."

"What? Why is it because you were already invited?"

"Nope I just don't know."

"Okay before you just say no can you think about it first?"

"Okay I will let you know later on this week."

"Alright later."

She was gone and left me in disbelief. She got my number without me and she asked me to be her date for the dance. I need something to clear my mind now. Letting my mom know I was going to Pat's house and I had my phone on me if she needed me. Making my way down the street to his house. I spoke to his mom and found him in his room playing video games. We are the same age but he looks younger than me. His boyish-like features kept him that way.

"What's up boy?"

I said breaking his concentration and for a split second having his attention. Looking at me smiling giving me a nod and then he was back to concentrating on his game.

"What's up brother?"

Pat asked me sounding concerned and he was right calling me brother, because Pat is like the brother I once had. Thinking about my brother Phillip really hurts, so I tried to avoid it at all causes.

"Guess who called me?" Trying not to give any emotions away.

"Crystal." He muttered excitedly.

"No man Stacey..."

Sounding as confused as I looked, however, I wish it was Crystal. He paused his game now having his undivided attention.

"Pretty Stacey called you?"

"Yes she called and asked me to a dance coming up at her school.

"I didn't know you gave her your number."

"Dude that's the thing, I didn't and I don't even know how she got my number." We both laughed.

"So ladies' man are you going to the dance?"

"I don't know."

"What do you mean? You don't know. Look man, when a girl Like Stacey asks for anything you don't say no." He paused in the middle of the conversation and looked puzzled.

"Please tell me your answer has nothing to do with my cousin."

Yes my answer has everything to do with his cousin. Strangely I can't believe he is on board about me going to the dance with Stacey.

"Well yes it does."

"But she's going to the dance with Derrick surely you can go with Stacey and you two are not even in a relationship."

Pat is right in so many ways, but I really care about Crystal and I have never felt this way for a girl before. I just know it's a bad idea showing up at the dance with Stacey.

"Anyway I think you should go and have fun."

I know I told Crystal to do the same thing, however, I just didn't think I'll be there to witness her having fun.

"Alright you're right it's just a dance I'll call her when I get back home."

"Why not call her now? I know you have your cell phone."

"Uh I don't have her number in my cell because she called the house phone." Looking up at me with an eyebrow raised in disbelief and spoke.

"Enough of this talking about girls, let's go play some ball."

Pat turned off the game and then put on his shoes and his jacket. Only if he knew playing ball was one of the main reasons for me coming over here, so when he suggested we play ball it was music to my ears.

CRYSTAL

Finally, we made it, and the building is an attention grabber with Lightly Fashion on top in lights, so it was kind of hard to miss. Inside Lightly Fashion was pretty much what I expected it to be, clothes, clothes, and more clothes. There was an older white haired woman at the counter. She confirmed our appointment and called a lady by the name of Sandy from the back. Sandy was much younger, probably in her middle twenties and so bubbly. Sandy introduced herself then she had us to follow her to a section where skirts and dresses took up most of the store.

"So many to choose from."

Cherish stated shopping was right up her alley. I bet she felt like a kid at a candy store. Rolling my eyes at her and pushing her arm.

"What Sunshine? Don't get mad at me because I actually like to shop."

There was no debating that because she did, furthermore I'm used to my momma shopping for me anyway. Whatever she bought I will wear it with no problem. Then again it's not like I had much of a choice, but this will be my first time picking out something that I actually will like. This was more nerve wrecking than I wanted it to be. I almost wanted to quit and let my momma pick out something, but I knew it will be unfair to Mika. I gave up, sat down and watched Mika and Cherish try on a dresses, because at this point I am done.

Cherish picked out one dress that was so short it would have given daddy a heart attack. Mika's butt is too big to wear anything short, and I knew I wasn't wearing anything short, so she can forget about a short dress. After they were done I guess it was my turn again. Searching through all these clothes everything started to look the same. While looking for something to wear I had to remind myself often looking at different pieces of clothing Mika and I will be dressed alike, so I had to consider her already developed chest. The first thing I picked out was a black sweet heart shaped neckline dress with diamonds around the chest part. I mean it was cute, but it said funeral not dance. I passed on that one, and there it was, something that could have been on a model in a magazine.

The dress is gorgeous; absolutely breathe taking. While admiring the dress I heard Mika say this was the one from behind me and I felt her excitement. The dress is an aqua sweet heart neckline jeweled dress with a tulle attached to it. The tulle is aqua and tan and is attached to a belt with a jeweled rose as the buckle. I couldn't believe all this time it was me who picked out our choice.

"Ms. Fay.... Ms. Fay Sunshine found us something to wear come and look."

Mika is too happy it was only a dress, but if I'm honest, I probably was happier than her for more than one reason, but I just didn't show any emotions. When my mom approached us I was holding the dress up in front of me on the hanger, so it was in plain sight. When she saw the dress she said it was beautiful placing her hands over her mouth. Cherish found a lime halter fitted mermaid dress that is light weight, which also has silver see through peek a boo sides, front splits, shear over it with sparkly stones at the top and it has a train that flared. Cherish' dress is beautiful also.

"Alright girls, show time."

My momma said directing us to the dressing room. I was so glad it was my first and the only dress I tried on. When we were in the dressing room, my mom brought us some shoes. When we all stepped out we were fully dressed. I came out last because I was feeling nervous and shy I didn't want them to see me.

"Sunshine if you don't come out I'm coming in there and you will not like it." So I complied regretfully because I didn't want my momma coming to get me.

Finally making it out the dressing room seeing Mika and Cherish in their dress left me speechless. I was in awe because they looked amazing and I was hoping I looked as good as them. They were in the full body mirrors and both of them were checking out their butts. My mom had met me at the door and led me to the mirrors and when the girls saw me they lost it. They were singing my praises on how beautiful I looked and the dress was gorgeous. Cherish had some silver heels that wrapped around her ankles, Mika had some aqua and tan heels that wrapped around her calves and I had some crystal slippers which was my first pair of heals. I was glad my shoes weren't high as Mika and Cherish, because I didn't want to fall and be scared for my life. Mika fixed her tulle so that it will be open, which will show off her fabulous legs and heels.

"Awe look at my babies you girls look stunning."

My momma said with a cracking voice, the one you get when you're trying not to cry, nevertheless, we said thank you still admiring ourselves in the mirror. The dress actually made me look like I had some breasts, so I was falling in love with the dress every time I viewed my reflection.

"Alright girls time to shut this fashion show down."

When my mom spoke you could still hear the admiration in her voice, so within me I felt good, because I picked the dresses out for Mika and me. We didn't argue we just did as she said. Mika paid for her own dress and my momma paid for mine and Cherish' things. Momma even picked out some matching jewelry for us all. She told Mika the jewelry was a gift for going to the next grade which made Mika even happier. I saw the way she hugged my mom saying thank you. I was trying to see how much everything cost, but my momma made it known it wasn't my business. On our way back to the car I asked if we can stop over at Auntie Cynthia's house.

"What's over at my sister's house?"

"Please mom you haven't seen her and I haven't seen my cousin."

I was pleading my case. It was true though all she did was talk to her, but she was always dealing with us or daddy she was homebound most of the times. She needed this break and I wanted to see Peter.

"Is Pat the only person you want to see?"

Cherish looked at me like she knew the answer, but I ignored her and waited on my momma's response.

"I haven't seen her in two weeks so I guess we will go visit."

My insides are jumping for joy having its own private Olympic tumbling show. Mika is looking at me smiling, but why is she smiling? I guess we've been friends long enough for her to know me. Mika figured it out I really wanted to see Peter especially since I haven't heard from him, so maybe I can find out what's going on with him even if he's not over my Auntie's house. The drive to her house was quiet and it felt shorter than the drive to Lightly Fashions. Mika went to sleep while her phone was charging, so I was left alone with all my ragging thoughts. When we came off the freeway closer to our destination, I felt my heart beat become rapid. I just knew my heart was about to beat out my chest and I couldn't help but to feel it was all because of Peter.

We pulled up to the house. Trying to pull myself together, I knew my calmness wouldn't last long especially if I see Peter. I woke up Mika and she did not look happy about it. Trying to change her mood I said.

"Yes, time to wake up sleeping beauty."

She started to smile so I accomplished my mission. Mika wasted no time in grabbing her cell phone and she had a missed message from her mom telling her she loved our dresses. Not only did my day start off good, it appeared to be ending well, which gave me a feeling of satisfaction. Momma knocked on auntie's door. When auntie answered she was so elated to see her because she skipped the formal how do you do, but grabbed her in her arms.

"Hey girls." She said acknowledging us and we all said hey.

"Auntie are you coming over to see me off to prom?"

"Baby yes, so that's why I'm not going to bother seeing your dresses you found today and I'm going to wait until the night, besides my sister is going to need as much help as she can get that night."

We all shared a moment of laughter. Her and my momma had coffee and a muffin and we had a turkey sandwich with some homemade punch, which is delicious. While eating, I realized I didn't hear Pat or Peter in the house and I am disappointed, but I tried not to show it or thought I wasn't showing disappointment on my face.

"Sunshine why are you looking like you lost your best friend?" My auntie's question hit me like a home run ball.

"Auntie I was looking forward to seeing my cousin and Pat's not here because I don't hear him."

All eyes were on me like they were having a staring contest, but I ignored their stares and focused on my auntie.

"Oh sweetie I just sent him and Peter to the store, they should be on their way back."

The mentioning of his name made my insides do cartwheels and as much as I wanted to do my best cheerleader scream and jump, I didn't.

"Okay can I go sit on the porch and wait since I'm done eating?"

She looked at my mom to get her approval and my mom agreed, so Mika and I went outside. Opening the door thinking I was in the clear, but it felt like I ran into a brick wall. I looked up to see it was Peter I bumped myself into and he was rubbing his chest, so the pain was mutual.

"Crystal."

He said looking surprised and shocked. I have to admit I was too, especially since he called me Crystal! I was trying to make as little eye contact as possible speaking and moving past him to reach Pat.

"Cousin!" I said wrapping my arms around him.

"Hey cousin, what's up how long will you be here?"

"I don't know, but my mom and your mom are in the kitchen talking you know, catching up in person.

"Alright then let me take my mom her stuff and I'll be right back."

Pat left us on the porch, and we stood there quietly only hearing the engine from the car across the street and the leaves as they danced to the beat of the wind.

"Hi, I'm Tamika Crystal's best friend, but friends call me Mika."

Mika announced herself with her hand stretched towards Peter, because clearly I was taking too long just another example of how Peter throws off my thinking.

"Nice to meet you Tamika, Crissy's best friend, so Crissy has a best friend that I knew nothing about?"

Peter says with a grin. Mika gave me a look but I couldn't read it, so I just hunched my shoulders

"Well now you know and it's better late than never, right?"

"I was wondering when my miss attitude was going to show up?"

Smirking he replied and if I did have an attitude it was because of him, but I didn't know why.

"Come on Crissy take a walk with me."

Grabbing for my hand being hesitant at first, but agreeing by placing my hand in his. While strolling off the porch looking back at Mika finding her smiling shaking her head up and down. All of a sudden, my hand felt hot in his hand which made me tense up and Peter must have felt it.

"Are you okay Crissy?"

"I don't know, but why did you ask?"

"Maybe because we're walking but your stiff as a board." We laughed.

"I only act like this when you're around me."

"So are you saying I make you nervous?"

"Yes that's exactly what I'm saying and I'm not sure if this is a bad or good thing."

Peter must have zoned out to a comedy club because he was laughing hysterically.

"You are so honest in your words and your body language is one of the main reasons I like you. I know I can count on you to tell me the truth even when you don't want to. With that being said, Crissy why won't you be my girlfriend?"

Stopping and he is standing over me and I'm looking up at his face and I can see the sincerity in his eyes, but what was I going to say?

"Peter it's not that I don't want to be your girlfriend."

"Yes, so you are saying that you will be my girlfriend?"

Peter's reaction revealed he was pleased with the thought of me being his girlfriend and I didn't want to rain on his parade, but I never agreed. What if I told him about my daddy's warning? Then he couldn't blame me and maybe he will understand, here goes nothing.

"Look Peter, my daddy said you are trouble and I refuse to get my feelings hurt."

I'm not sure what I said, but his demeanor wasn't jocular but serious. I see the tightness of his cheek bones and he's staring off in space. For a split second I regretted I had said anything. My plan was not to hurt his feelings with my truth, this is all bad. I called his name twice before snapping him out of space.

"Yes Crystal."

He says forcefully. Perfect, now I'm back to Crystal he must be mad and it's still my fault the very thing I was trying to avoid is happening right now. Can we say my plans backfired?

"So I guess I'm going to be Crystal from now on?

With a playful smile, I pouted my lip and with my head tilted to the side, I asked him. The muscles in his face started to relax and he smiles.

"Come on let us get back to your auntie's house."

We trotted back down the street to the porch and found Mika and Pat on the porch. They were too close if you ask me, but I thought nothing else of it.

"They're back, how is the happy couple?"

I could feel Peter tensing up next to me but said nothing and shook his head from side to side. Mika gave me a puzzled look like she missed something. I was holding my head down so she couldn't read me like a physic on a good day.

"Alright Pat I just remembered I have something to handle for my mom I'll get at you later."

Tamika and Crissy nodding his head saying goodbye and just like that he was gone.

"Sunshine you didn't tell me your cousin was cute and so funny."

"I'm not that funny but I am cute." We all laughed.

"If you say so?"

I mean I never thought of Pat as cute or funny, he is my cousin who I love and he is fun to hang with. Now I was ready to go coming over here didn't go as planned. Sure I saw Peter, but now I'm not sure what to think about him. I just know there was a ton of questions roaming free in my brain. I went back inside and left Pat and Mika on the porch.

"Sunshine now what's wrong I thought you wanted to see Pat?" I never was good at keeping my emotions off my face. If I was happy, sad, mad, hurt you could see it and there was no hiding it. Sighing.

"Boys why are they so complicated?" I couldn't believe I actually asked that question out loud, but oh well, I can't take it back now.

"Auntie I did see Pat."

"What did he do to get under your skin?"

"Auntie it's not Pat under her skin, but Peter."

Leave it to Cherish to a get a good laugh at my expense. Now she added to my frustration and I really was ready to leave. Sometimes I didn't know who had the biggest mouth Michael or Cherish. Finally, I heard my mom say I better head back to the house. I never thought I'll be so elated to go home maybe I just wanted to be as far away from Peter as possible.

PETER

Man I cannot believe Crystal; she won't even get to know me or give me a chance because of her dad. No, not her dad but my dad. Leaving was the best thing to do at the moment running is the next best thing to basketball when it comes to taking my mind off situations. Now my feet are throbbing and my legs are exhausted alone. I'm sitting at the table trying to do my homework and it's hard to concentrate between the pain in my legs from jogging and the pain in my heart from Crystal's rejection. At this point, I don't know which one is worse.

The sound of the house phone ringing jolted me out of my thoughts. Hearing the voice on the other end, I instantly became irritated resentment filled my heart and I hated when he called my mom. Sometimes I wish he was locked up with my father. I know it may be a horrible way to feel, but Rich was tall dark and evil. Sure he and dad had some underground connections, but now that dad is locked up why is he continuing to bother us?

"Mom, telephone."

Yelling to her from the kitchen. The way she came in the kitchen smiling she must have thought it was daddy. When she realized it wasn't him that smile she wore on her face like a summer blouse disappeared like a magician's rabbit in a hat trick. While on the phone, my mom barley said a word, however, her facial expressions were saying enough and it took everything in me not to hang up. Their conversation lasted five minutes, but felt like a lifetime. As soon as she placed the phone down I drilled her with questions.

"Mom why does he keep calling?"

"Baby it's complicated and you wouldn't understand." She was so calm but just like she knew me; I knew her also.

"Bull."

Slamming my fist in my hand, but before I could even finish she intercepted the conversation with a higher tone in her voice and her eyes popping out the sockets. I knew I went too far and I had to fix it.

"You watch your mouth when you are talking to me do you understand me?"

"Momma I'm sorry I just want to help, but I can't if I don't know what's going on?"

"When your daddy was out he hooked up with a lot of horrible people and that's all I'm saying right now." I guess I had to respect that at least she said that much.

"Mom I was invited to Bailey High's last dance." Trying to change the subject and the tension in the room. She looked surprised.

"By who, Crystal?" I wish it was Crystal, I couldn't lie to her I had to tell her the truth and be prepared for her brutal response.

"No it wasn't her, but in my defense I would rather it be her."

"Are you going?"

"I'm thinking about it."

"Well since you're telling me you must want to know what I think and I think you should go, not only that, but enjoy yourself."

I can honestly say I wasn't expecting her to be so cool with the idea.

"What's her name?"

"Stacey." I said giving my best confused smile look.

"Okay you need to let her know and see what she is wearing, so when can get you together?"

"Thanks mom you know you're really not that bad of a woman."

Joking making her smile from her heart. Knowing I had taken her mind off that awful Rich, but this is not over I'm going to find out why he keep` calling us. First things first, let me call Stacey to tell her the good news. Making the phone call thinking that I was glad I talked to my mom about this ordeal. Hanging up with Stacey I dialed Crystal's number, stared at it contemplating if I should hit send and call her. Letting my nerves get the best of me I closed the phone and put it on my stand. Turning on my TV to the sports channel watching sports until I fall asleep are my plans.

CRYSTAL

The drive back home was quick and quite, neither one of us said anything, which was fine with me. I mean I had Peter on the brain lately he is all I thought about. Sometimes I would ask myself how did this happen? The number one question that flows through my head like loose cannons is what my dad knows about Peter that made him believe he is trouble. I couldn't figure it out; however, I planned on finding out. Dropping Mika off in front of her house, so she wouldn't have to walk down the street carrying her dress. We said our goodnights and it was our time to head home. At home, dad had already prepared dinner him and Michael and it smelled good, or maybe I am starving and anything would have smelled good.

Dinner was good just like I wanted it to be, the taste matched the smell and surprisingly shocking especially since the men folk made dinner. Daddy saw our dresses and he loved them even though he wasn't too happy with Cherish' peek a boo sides, but he still approved. Michael and daddy had made plans to go shopping also and look for something to wear for Michael. In my room I surfed through the channels and nothing was catching my attention. I decided to take a hot bath, everybody else was winding down. Running the water like I usually do letting the bathroom steam up just like I enjoyed it. Placing my towel on the shower pole and having the urge to find out if Peter was alright. Turning off the water, I tip toed downstairs trying to be discreet and quiet, but having wood floors made it challenging. Downstairs mom was in the twins' room in the big chair I assumed. I got Peter's number off our caller ID. I was more nervous than I had ever been debating if I should call, but I came this far I may as well. The phone rang three times before he answered.

"Hello." His voice was deeper than I'd ever heard it before and the sound sent an unexplainable feeling in my stomach.

"Hey Peter, it's Crystal I was just calling to check on you." If you were sleeping I can always call you back.

"Yea I was sleep, but you're good. Let me get this straight, little miss attitude was concerned about me, the trouble maker?" Sarcasm, typical Peter.

"I guess I had that coming."

"I'm okay, so now that you know I'm okay what's next?" What did he mean? I don't know I haven't thought that far into calling him.

"If it means anything, I'm glad you are okay and I'm sorry for everything."

"Crissy, why are you apologizing?"

I was apologizing, because I felt bad for everything from not answering his question about me being his girlfriend, going to the dance with Derrick and most of all, telling him my dad thinks he's trouble. Before I could answer my other line started to ring, so I told Peter hold on I had to answer it.

"Hello." The voice was husky, so I knew it was Uncle Richard.

"Hey Uncle Richard, but my daddy's not here I'll tell him you called.

"Actually Sunshine, I wanted you."

Me what could he possibly want with me? I know we are family he's my dad's younger brother, but the most we ever do is speak, so I'm startled at this point.

"Me, but why me?"

"Calm down Sunshine it won't be bad unless you make it bad. I know about your new boyfriend and it's really not a good idea for you to continue to talk to him."

I became angry and not liking this conversation not one bit. The nerve of him he is not my daddy and besides his brother already gave me a warning. What is this, gang up on Peter? Whatever it was Peter is my friend and if I stopped talking to him it will be my choice.

"Okay Uncle I get it, also I've already heard this speech from my daddy and honestly I don't need to hear it from you." I couldn't believe I said that, I may as well prepare myself mentally for some form of punishment.

"Girl that mouth and attitude of yours is going to get you in trouble one day momma and daddy can't save you from." Uncle or not, was he threatening me? It was time to go before I said anything else to fuel his fire against Peter and me.

"Alright Uncle I appreciate the concern I'll take everything you said into consideration bye bye talk to you later."

"No see you soon."

That was really weird what did he mean he will see me soon? What if I didn't want to see him at all? Shaking that entire conversation off clicking back over Peter was still there. I was surprised, because if it was me I would have hung up.

"Sorry again that was my Uncle Richard." Abruptly he responded.

"Rich is your Uncle? Tall dark and husky voice?" He asks, but how did he know who he was?

"Yep that's him, but how do you know him?"

"I don't, I just know of him and I think he knows my dad." He never mentioned his Dad before, just his mom and brother. This is a first.

"Who is your dad?"

CHAPTER 5

"My dad is Peter Jackson; you may have seen him on the news a few years ago as Underground Peter Jackson." It sounded familiar but I couldn't put my finger on it though.

"Sounds familiar, but I'm not sure."

"Alright Crissy, I have to go thanks for checking on me talk to you later."

He was gone and I couldn't say anything. I wonder what that was about; nevertheless I took a hot shower instead of a bubble bath. I was drained emotionally and had a lot of things to wrap my head around. The shower was still relaxing and just what the doctor ordered.

Dear Journal,
We all found dresses thank God ones that we all are happy with. I saw Peter today I was really excited to see him even if I didn't show it. I told him my dad said he's trouble. I believe those words hurt his feelings, but I couldn't take them back and it was too late. Calling him was my attempt to make things right epic fail, because I still didn't know where we stood.

PETER

I was shocked to hear from Crissy and it was a wonderful surprise to wake up to her sweet voice on the other end of my phone. Maybe she cares after all, but I couldn't forget about the information I just learned. Crissy is the niece of Mr. Evil himself Rich. Crissy's Father is a cop and her Uncle is a criminal, it was a lot to accept. Laying back down attempting to get comfortable, my mind is still thinking about the recent discoveries. I was sleepy and tired of thinking turning on some music to help relax me and eventually I fell asleep.

Where am I? Who are you? Sitting here in a slightly dim room with my hands and feet bound with handcuffs to a metal chair. A man's back is the only thing that can be seen. Grunting mixed with heavy breathing trying to break free and yelling let me go. Finally, shaking the chair which got the attention of the man turning facing my way and I couldn't believe my eyes. It is Sheriff Hartland, the door opened and the light shined so bright it could have been heaven on the other side, but when I saw who came through the door I knew it wasn't heaven. The light was only decoration. It was Rich with a bat in his hand and when he closed the door the room was back dim.

"Brother Look who I found walking my baby Sunshine home, I warned her about him she didn't listen, so I think we need to teach him a lesson."

"Yea the same lesson I taught his daddy."

Walking towards me feeling myself becoming furious and my heart rate soared to a new height. I couldn't believe he was coming towards me with a bat or that he mentioned he did something to my daddy. When he was close enough I used all my strength and I threw myself at him. Falling back on the floor and opening my eyes realizing I was back in my room on my bed. That dream left me in a pile of sweat. I looked at my phone to see it was 8 a.m. in the morning. It was too early for Pat to be to be awake unless he's going to church, but I didn't want to call down there to find out, so I'll just get at him later. After showering, I got dressed and made my way to the kitchen.

Making my way to the kitchen I grabbed a banana and poured a glass of orange juice. My momma made eggs oatmeal and turkey bacon. The way I was about to run I needed everything for energy. She finally made her way to the kitchen and the first thing I noticed she had on makeup which she doesn't wear often, so I wanted to know what was the special occasion. The way her jeans hugged her hips and her purple blouse embraced her chest I knew something was up.

"Good morning pretty lady where are you going?" Giving my most innocent smile.

"Hey love you're up early on a Sunday." I couldn't help remembering my dream, the reason for me being up so early.

"Who you telling I had a nightmare."

Thinking of it sent goose bumps down my arms. She laughs and stared at me immensely. I didn't know which was worse her laughing or her staring. I had to change the subject the thought of reliving that dream was unbearable.

"So mom, what are your plans?

"I'm going to visit your father maybe you should join me?"

She knew I will say no it was a distraction for me not to think deep into her visiting him out of the blue because usually she will give me a chance to think about it knowing the answer will be no. I knew this had something to do with Rich calling her. I didn't want to really know if I was right because either way it went I wasn't going to be happy with her answer.

"Momma did you know Crystal is Rich' niece?"

There was a long pause as if she was debating on how to answer my question, but because of her pause, I already knew the answer to my question.

"Baby there's a lot of things I know, but I can't share them right now."

What does she mean? And why can't I know? Frustrating as this conversation was becoming, I wanted to get as much information out of her as I could.

"Things like what mom? What can't I know now and when will be the right time?"

The look on her face displayed the conviction in her heart keeping things from me, because we usually talked about any and everything. What made this so different?

"Peter I'm sorry, but this is the way it has to be for now and I've already said too much."

Grabbing my face as gently as she could and looking me dead in my eyes. She walked out the kitchen to the front door not saying another word. This was too much to digest. I finished my breakfast and went jogging. Thinking about my dream, thinking about the conversation I had with my mom, but most of all, thinking about Crissy. During the jog I made it up in my mind I was going to revisit my dad's case and see if I can connect the dots. Why would Mr. Hartland tell Crissy I'm trouble and why does Mr. Hartland's criminal brother keep calling my house? Finally, making it back to my house sitting on the porch drowning in sweat. I was enjoying the spring breeze until my phone started to ring. I didn't recognize the number, so I didn't answer it.

I was at the park longer than I expected, but it gave me time to think. I thought about my brother if he was here how different things could be. I blamed my dad for a long time for his accident. I often felt like him going to prison was some kind of payback for me. I may have been young when it happened, but I can still remember those nights my momma cried herself to sleep and when she made me stay in the house for months. The only time I was allowed out was when she was with me, so I'm glad that's over with. The shower and the jog was relaxing I decided to chill at the crib all day and I wanted to be here when my momma came back home. Fixing me a homemade sub sandwich which was on point. Homemade food is always better than cook out food to me. Sitting here eating thinking about how I needed something to wear to the dance. Maybe mom and I can go grab something when she gets back. I guess I spoke her up I heard her keys at the door. She smiled when she saw me, so that had to mean she had a good visit.

"Hey love, I'm surprised to see you here I just knew you would be gone."

"Nope well I went to the park jogged longer than I planned, but it was needed, and I'm glad you came back kind of early."

"Oh yeah is that right? What you got up your sleeves son?"

"Nothing really mom, you know this dance coming up and we haven't been shopping yet."

"That's it boy I thought you was about to tell me you're in love or something else boy you almost gave me a mini heart attack." We both laughed. I knew I wasn't in love yet, but if my feelings keep growing for Crystal I will be.

"Alright we're out."

She grabbed a banana I see how excited she is and it felt good seeing her so happy. The drive was at least 20 minutes we had to shop outside of Bay City. My mom was an old school head that's all she listened too. I mean hits from the 60s, 70s and the 80s she was on it and didn't care what we thought. One of the things I admire about her is that she wears her game face all the time. We were quite the ride to Raids Fashions and I thought about how I wished Pat was with me, however, I was happy with just the two of us. She worked a lot even on her off days if she was called in she would go in to work if they needed her.

We finally pulled up to Raids Fashions inside a strip mall and man this place is packed. I don't like big crowds I almost want to turn around, but it wouldn't be fair to mom to come this far for nothing, so I sucked it up. The outside wasn't so spectacular like Lightly Fashions which was crazy because they shared the same owner. The inside was suits galore. I love putting clothes together, so this will be a piece of cake. The greeter was an older man with salt and pepper hair very welcoming. Thanks for choosing Raids Fashion where our clothes kill every occasion and he led us to the back of the store. I tried on suits on top of suits. I knew Stacey was wearing white so looking for something that matches will be easy.

My momma was having too much fun watching me dress up, her excitement never left since we left the house. I tried on this blue and white suit checking myself out in the mirror she came from behind me with tears in her eyes.

"Baby you look good and your daddy would be so happy to see you dressed up like this!"

Honestly I had no response for her I watched her smile slowly fade away when I paused, but it wasn't because of her or him. I had to make her smile again.

"Well I get it from daddy." Speaking while adjusting my bowtie and there it was, that smile I wanted to see.

"So I have no part in you looking good?"

Dusting off my shoulders we laughed. Becoming annoyed, because I haven't come across something that made me wanted to buy it nothing is grabbing my attention. Starting to feel like I've been in this store long enough and was about to give up until my eyes came across an aqua and white dressy suit and converse outfit. I think I found a winner. I tried on everything even the shoes. I stepped out the dressing room and the expression on my mom's face is priceless, I knew this outfit was the one.

"'Awe baby you must get this one."

Still checking it out in the mirror, I think she's right this is the one I'm buying. My shoes were on point some all-white converse with aqua soles and shoe strings. While my mom was paying for the clothes, my phone started to ring and it was that same number I didn't recognize, so I didn't answer it. Who could this be? And why aren't they leaving me a voicemail?

"You ready son?"

"Let's roll out."

Walking out the door I held it opened for her just like she taught me when I was younger. She was pleased. My stomach started to growl and it was time to eat again.

"Mom can we go out to eat for dinner?"

We don't go often, so I was hoping she would say yes without a great debate. Plus I haven't forgotten about our conversation from earlier and this will give us a chance to finish what I started.

"Sure, where to?"

That was easy and quick she must really be in a good mood, but I haven't thought that far concerning what I wanted to eat. I didn't want hamburgers, fries, pizza or chicken.

"What about Bay Hong?" It was closer to home and good food.

"Chinese?" She asks hesitantly, I saw her thinking about it.

"Alright I guess I can use some pepper steak and rice."

"Yes."

Placing my hand up for a hive five. On the way to Bay Hong we weren't quiet we were having our own personal concert. She will sing a part then me and we both sung the chorus. We were there in no time. The place wasn't so crowed by the time we arrived I was surprised, because it was Sunday one of their busiest days. The first person who met us only asked us a question.

"You dine in?"

Smiling we said yes nodding our heads also. She gave us instruction to follow her, by nodding her head and using her hand signaling for us to follow her. The restaurant had small red and orange lanterns hanging up all over the building. The Lanterns that are hanging up over the table are bigger and lit up. It is really unique, a touch of their home in our city. As soon as we sat down we were ready to order. We didn't even use a menu because we already made up our mind in the car. We both order pepper steak with Wu-tang soup. The waitress who took our order is much younger than our greeter. She was surprised to see we were ready so quick. Fifteen minutes she told us walking away smiling.

Alright it's now or never. It was time she is relaxed and comfortable and she didn't even take her phone out her purse, so I knew I would have her undivided attention.

"So how is he?" In my best concerned voice hitting her with the first question.

"He's okay, but he misses his son."

She pouted her lips playfully, but I knew it was true because I missed my dad also. I knew it was time for a visit, but as I got older it hurts badly to see him in there. I do write to him and talk to him when he calls home, but I guess it's not enough for him.

"I know momma, believe it or not I miss him also and I'm planning to go see him soon." Actually this conversation will depend on how soon that will be.

"He wants you to attend the dance and enjoy yourself."

"You told him, so did you also tell him about my date and Crystal?" I was annoyed because I wanted to tell him.

"Well did you tell him Rich keeps calling?" Sounding harsh, because looking at her face I see I hit a nerve. Man I need to learn how to control my temper.

"Of course I did, I told him everything I felt he needed to know. Are you happy now?"

"Well what did he say?"

Not sure if I was ready for her answer bracing myself mentally for the impact of her answer. Before she had a chance to speak, the waitress was placing our food on the table it broke up the tension between us, but this was far from over, as a matter a fact, this waitress wasn't moving fast enough.

"Okay mom now we can talk and eat, so what did he say?"

"Baby I know how you feel about Crystal please keep in mind she has nothing to do with what you are about to learn. Once you open this door there's no closing it."

The sincerity in her eyes sent a verbal punch in my rib cage and I was struggling to breath. Finally, catching my breath in and out I was coaching myself on breathing in my mind.

"Mom." I pleaded sounding desperate and she still was stalling.

"I'm going to make a long story short. Rich and your dad did business together. When your daddy became popular in the streets Rich became jealous and he wanted him eliminated, but he didn't want to kill him, your daddy was more valuable alive at the time, so he framed him."

"Momma are you saying he's innocent?" Slamming my fist on the table.

"That's not what I'm saying. The stolen merchandise was stolen by your daddy all 100,000 dollars' worth. That he did, but he never killed anybody." Maybe she was right I should've left that door closed.

"But what do Crystal and her dad has to do with any of this besides it's his brother and her uncle?"

There was a heavy sigh before she replied. I seriously didn't know how much more of this mental beat down I can handle, but I had to know.

"Mr. Hartland knows the truth, but Rich uses his kids against him."

That was the straw that broke the camel's back and before I knew it I was standing up over my momma with anger in my heart and revenge in my head.

"Peter Jafarr Jackson sit your tail down right now."

She charges me firmly and I knew she was serious. I listened, but before I did I saw the attention I had drawn with my actions, and these people are looking terrified.

"Scene one take one angry kid."

While taking a bow repeatedly and clapping my hands. By this time my mom caught on she started to yell bravo clapping her hands and finally some spectators joined in. That was my cue to take my seat. Leave it up to me making a serious and tense scene comical. Looking around there were smiles on people's faces mixed with confusion, but at least they weren't going to call the cops on me. Focusing back on my mom she even found it humorous.

"Mom he can't get away with this."

"We know it's just at the moment our hands are tied and when your dad was first locked up I thought I could trust Rich, but I was so wrong. He must not know that we know the truth. You got that? He is a very dangerous man and can't be trusted."

I felt sorry for my daddy being framed for murder, I felt sorry for Mr. Hartland having a criminal as a brother, and I felt sorry for Crystal, because I felt utterly helpless.

"So you expect me to keep this a secret?"

"If Rich finds out we know, he will come after the both of us and Crystal and her family."

Freezing up because my phone started to ring checking it and it was that number again. I told my mom it's the third time today she instructed me to answer it, I complied.

"Yea."

Was my only response, but I recognized the voice and I couldn't believe he was calling my cell phone. My free fist started to ball up. My mom noticed she asked who was it, but no words came out her mouth. Rich I said without mumbling a sound, but visible so she could read my lips. She nodded her head giving me the okay to carry on.

"You pretty hard to catch up with."

"Nope I wouldn't say that I just don't answer numbers I don't know, besides you have the house number, you didn't call because I was there most of the day."

"What's up?" I had to ask feeling like I was doing too much talking.

"Anxious are we?" Of course the sooner I knew why he was calling me the quicker I can get off the phone with him.

"I hear you have a thing for my niece, but you're going to the dance with Stacey."

Man if my mom wasn't here I'll be cussing like a sailor, but keeping my cool, because I didn't want to cause another scene they are not asking for an encore.

"Actually, Rich one out of two is right and not that I owe you an explanation, but I want you to know the truth. Yes, I had a thing for your niece, but as of yesterday we decided it wasn't a good idea for us to talk and that's when I agreed to attend the dance with Stacey."

I knew I was lying, but if it meant protecting Crystal, I'll lie again.

"You just don't know how happy I am to hear that, because if my niece was getting hurt it will be by me and not some punk." I can't believe what I'm hearing he's not evil he's the devil in the flesh.

"Alright are we done?" Agitated as I was I should have hung up in his face, but there is no need to add fuel to the fire.

"Boy we are done when I say we are done and we are done."

The line is dead and he was gone. Enough of this, I'm ready to go home. We called for the waiter asking for a carry out. When she brought the carry out, my mom paid we packed what was left and headed home finally. The drive home is quiet and full of blank stares. School was tomorrow, I had gym second hour which was a blessing at this point, because I had a lot of steam to blow off and I knew I wouldn't make it to the park until after school.

While sitting in my room on my bed feeling like someone dumped a ton of cement on my chest, I didn't know how to release the pressure that is on me. Thinking about Crystal and how jacked up it had to be being related to something so evil. Mr. Hartland should've been warning her about her uncle instead of me. I knew if I stuck to the story I told Rich staying away from Crystal I could keep her safe. Trying to figure out how he knew so much about my personal life is baffling, because I knew I didn't give him an invite to my personal life, but yet he still knew. Nobody knew about Stacey and me, but Stacey and Pat. I don't want to believe that either one of them had dealings with someone so evil. Thinking of Pat, I haven't heard from him today.

Trying to take my mind off of Rich and his deviant behavior, I turned on the TV looking for something to watch that will make me laugh. I came across a marathon of Americas Home Funniest Videos, so I watched it. This show is nothing new to me, as a matter of fact; we all used to watch it together before Phillip died. Americas Home Funniest Videos was the one show that brought me, mom, dad and my brother together and we shared so many laughs watching this show. We tried to recreate certain videos from the show just for laughs, but now I understand we were creating memories for me.

An hour into one of the shows, I knew it did the trick because I started to feel better. Laughing until my stomach started hurting and I am trying not to disturb my momma, because I know she is preparing for bed. I hated commercials so I started channeling surfing and came across an FBI advertisement for school trying to recruit people. The part that tickled my fancy is when they talked about phone tapping. I immediately grab my cell off the bed and researched phone tapping. The first thing that popped up was different devices that are used. My mind was racing, why would Rich Tap our phone? Then it hit me like a bolt of lightning, he wanted to know how much we knew about him and what he did, so he has been listening to us the entire time. Running to my mom's room to tell her my theory. I was glad to see she is still up.

"Mom question, what if Rich has been listening to us the entire time dad has been locked up?" For the first time, I saw fear in mother's eyes grabbing her chest.

"What makes you think that?" She muttered dryly.

"Mom he knows about me going to the dance with Stacey and how I feel about Crystal. I called Crystal from the house phone a few times and Stacey called me on the house phone. Plus I only told Pat you and Stacey about the dance over the phone, but yet he knows. Noticing the concern on her face as she was considering everything I said.

"Baby you may be on to something, but why?"

"Mom do you really not know. He wants to know if we knew what he did." There was silence before she said anything else. I knew right then she knew it was possible.

"So what do you suggest we do?"

I can't believe what I'm hearing; she's actually asking me for help this was more serious than I was thinking. In my take charge voice.

"First things first we get rid of the house phone and get a new number."

"But your dad will worry if he calls and gets no answer, because it will take a day or two before we receive the new number."

She was right; the last thing I wanted him to do was worry about us. I had to think of something.

"I know what if you get off work early we can go visit him."

She smiled a smile that made my heart melt. I knew she is smiling because I was agreeing to go visit my dad.

"It's a date." High fiving me.

We both go to the kitchen to unhook the house phone. Just out of curiosity I busted the phone open to see if I will find anything, and what do you know, there it is a piece of metal that was different from the other debris from the phone, so this had to be it. I took a hammer from the dresser and smashed it on the table. We exhale with relief, then my phone started to ring and we jumped because it startled the both of us. What was worse is that it was Rich, I recognized the number this time, but I didn't answer. I was shaking my head no to my mom and she was staring looking emotionless. Rich calling was the proof I needed it is true he's been listening to us on the house phone. He had my cell number, but he had never been alone with my cell phone like he has been with our house phone to plant a bug. This just kept getting crazier by the moment which left my head spinning.

"Now mom, don't be surprised if he pops up over here."

We needed to have a believable story together and have it ready for him just in case, because there was no doubt in my mind he is not coming.

"Oh that's easy, we can tell him we broke it problem solved."

She laughs. In that moment I realized I am like her in more ways than one, but I was the split image of my daddy. Phillip looked like both our parents. I can't remember which one he acted like, but I can remember how much fun it was playing with him. Mom and I both had our cell phones, so if there was an emergency we had an outlet to the authorities. We kissed on the cheek she gave me a bear hug said goodnight and we went to our rooms. Back where I started back on my bed. This time I have no desire to watch TV, so I just took a hot shower put me on a white beater a pair of shorts and called it night. I turned on some music laid horizontal on my bed and relaxed until I fell asleep.

CRYSTAL

Man, church was hype it took my mind away from all the drama in my life, but now it's over and my thoughts are on a rampage. I wanted to call Peter, but the warnings I received were on repeat in my head. I still couldn't figure out what Uncle Richard had to do with anything and I couldn't ask my daddy, because he wouldn't be able to let it go. I haven't heard from Mika today which was strange and as much as I didn't feel like going downstairs to call her, I knew I had to find out what was going on with her? The house was quiet. Daddy was gone and momma was in her room tonight.

Calling Mika's cell phone instead of her house phone, because she had it back and it was late to call the house phone. Getting ready to hang up, but she answered on the third ring.

"Hey girl what's up?"

"Nothing what you mean what's up?"

Whoa I was not expecting that reaction or in that aggravated tone. She was only like this during her period which I have yet to see for myself or she is trying to keep me from knowing something.

"Girl don't be giving me no attitude I know you are not on your period, so what's with the attitude?" She paused and she is usually quick with a rebuttal, so I knew it was more and I waited.

"What do you want me to say?" She was laying the attitude on thick.

"Girl don't make me come down there. Why haven't I heard from you today and don't give me you been busy, because I will not believe it one bit."

"Well I was kind of busy." Dryly she muttered.

"With who James?"

"No not with James."

She was more relaxed I heard it in her tone. This is about to be interesting, so I kicked my feet up on the couch wishing I had snacks for this conversation.

"Then who?" That question shot out my mouth like a stray bullet and she laughed, but I was so serious.

"Sunshine don't be mad I wasn't going to tell you because I didn't want this to come between our friendship."

Now she is starting to scare me. Holding my breath while I sat back up on the edge of the couch preparing for the worse.

"Mika for crying out loud spit it out who was he?"

"Patrick."

"Patrick." I repeated sounding like a broken record. I started laughing uncontrollably and I couldn't help it.

"Okay you can stop laughing now." I couldn't help it this is hilarious and I was laughing so hard tears started to flow.

"Sunshine if you don't stop laughing I'm hanging up."

"Mika don't hang up I'm sorry it's just this has shocked the crap out of me." I guess she wasn't playing when she said he was cute.

"But when? How?" I asked, because if she thought that was the end of the conversation she had another thing coming.

"When you and Peter went for a walk we talked and exchanged numbers we've been texting and talking ever since."

"But I saw him in church and he didn't say anything."

"Because I asked him not to. I wanted to be the one to tell you."

"What about James?" I felt like the paparazzi getting a hot story, but I had to know, also I didn't want my cousin to be hurt by Mika's shenanigans.

"Well he knows about James and he said it wouldn't be fair to cancel at the last minute."

"Wow that was very mature of him."

"Don't stop there, he actually told me to have fun and enjoy myself."

"Yep he and Peter are definitely friends." We both laughed and there was this awkward silence between us. Something that doesn't happen often, but I couldn't help but to realize she may have seen Peter.

"No Sunshine."

"No What Mika?" I knew she knew what I was thinking about especially since I knew where she was at.

"Peter was not there. As a matter of fact, he hadn't even spoken with him the entire time I was there."

I felt sad, because at the moment Mika is the only connection I had with Peter being so close to him today.

"Well that's why I was calling you, because while on the phone with Peter, my Uncle Richard called and told me to stay away from Peter."

"I don't know sunshine maybe they know something you don't"

"That's obvious Mika, but what they know is the question!"

"When I told Peter my dad said he is trouble, he was hurt Mika and I wanted to hug his hurt away at least try to make him feel better."

"That's why he left so quickly when you guys returned back to the house."

"Yea I know and I wished he didn't though maybe we could've talked more and now I don't know what to think."

"If it makes you feel any better I know when a guy likes a girl trust me. I read enough books and magazines and Peter really likes you a lot Sunshine."

I was glad she thought so and it did make me feel a little better. She started yawing, so I took the hint.

"Alright Mika go to sleep sleeping beauty and thanks for everything"

"No problem sunshine goodnight."

CHAPTER 6

Mika could barely get her words out before another yawn attacked her mouth, nevertheless she was gone. Trying to make some sense of Uncle Richard and his warning, but I came up with nothing and it really is disturbing me. Sitting on the couch thinking, but in my case, over thinking. Why the first guy I like has to come with so much confusion and drama. Why couldn't it be more simplified? Simple was the last thing I remembered before falling asleep on the couch.

Peter screaming his name over and over, but he just kept running and eventually he was out of sight. I wanted to try so desperately to find out what and who he was running from, but first I had to find out where was I. Wandering around in what appeared to be a building. The place is lit up which made it easier for me to see, so I sashayed down the hall calmly.

Reaching the end of the hallway there is three doors to choose from, but which one to pick. Since I don't like odd numbers I picked number two. Opening the door finding a dark room. Instantly regretting my choice at that very moment, but I couldn't choose again, because the other doors had disappeared. Going through door number two was my only option, and I couldn't even go back down the hallway, because that path was gone. Fear sat in my heart which is racing and I started to sweat feeling it coming down my cheeks like tears. Right before walking through the door, I heard my daddy calling my name from a distance. I woke up and realized it was just a dream and my daddy was sitting next to me calling my name to wake me up.

"Hey dad."

"Hey Sunshine some kind of dream you were having?" Oh no what did he hear me say?

"Why you say that?" Wiping the crust from my eyes.

"I tried to wake you up three times and you didn't even budge.

"Just tired I guess."

"Ok Sunshine go upstairs and get in the bed."

Following his instruction and glad I had already showered flopping in my bed and I was out for the count. The next morning, after I got dressed for school I went downstairs to join my family and I couldn't believe my eyes. Uncle Richard was sitting at the table having breakfast. I had to act like I'm not disturbed by his presence even when I'm highly irritated by the thought of him. Speaking to everyone including Uncle Richard. Why did he have to be the one to give me my first response?

"There she is my favorite niece."

His husky voice and his poisonous words sent chills down my arm. I felt like ignoring him, but I knew ignoring him will be asking for a punishment for being rude towards a grown-up.

"Good morning." My voice was wobbly trying to hide how frightened I actually am, but failed.

Suddenly losing my appetite, I grabbed a banana from the table and sat on the couch.

"Sunshine are you feeling okay?"

Hearing the concern in my mom's voice and finding my daddy eyes staring immensely at me answering cautiously.

"Yea I just had a bad dream and fell asleep downstairs last night."

My daddy intervened and confirmed my story. I laid my head back on the couch and sighed. When is he leaving and why is he here? This whole situation is making me nervous. *Oh snap here he comes.* He sat down next to me and I tensed up, but no one seemed to notice he had left the table.

"Guess who's taking you to school?"

Why's he whispering? This is can't be true because nobody ever takes us to school but my momma or daddy. Something definitely didn't feel right about this idea. He threatened me for crying out loud, so what makes him think I trust him. I started to think of excuses to stay home. I couldn't stay home because I had to meet up with Derrick and tell him about the dress, so he would have an idea on what to wear. This sucks so bad not having a cell phone, but one day I will.

Everyone was wrapping it up and I realized he was telling the truth. Kissing my mom and dad goodbye, but I was hoping my daddy felt the tension in my body language. I wanted so bad to have a meeting in the lion's den. Maybe I'm making a big deal out of nothing, maybe it was all in my head with just a couple of questions that flooded my mind. Daddy drove the younger ones and Uncle Richard drove us to school. Making it my business to sit in the back, which came back to haunt me, because when everyone scuffed out the car I was stuck in the car with him.

"Not so fast Sunshine."

Aw man here we go. I needed a reason to get out this car and what's worse my stupid sisters and brother hadn't noticed I still was in the car. They were swept away in the crowd.

"Uncle Richard I'm going to be late for class."

"Little girl do you think I care, so now you have no other choice to hear what I have to say."

It felt like he shot a dagger straight to the core of my emotions. I mean why is he so cold towards me and what did I ever do to him? Starting to pity myself as if I was in the wrong. To make this as quick as possible I tried my best not to fight him anymore.

"You have my attention."

"I know I told you over the phone to stay away from Peter, but something tells me you didn't get the message, so here I am telling you in person to make it clear. Stay as far as you can away from Peter Jackson, or I will make you."

Now I'm bothered, but I don't know which one was worse. The fact he knew his first and last name or that he was threatening me again. Slowly moving closer to the door creating more distance between us.

"Uncle is this really necessary? I heard what you said the first time. Trust me I understand, but I also know I don't like you threatening me. As a matter of fact, I wonder how my daddy will feel if he knew you'd been threatening me?"

He laughed the most sinister laugh I have ever heard.

"Girl please I will drop that jolly green giant and whoever else gets in my way."

Seeing something in his eyes I had never seen in nobody eyes before was pure evil. Considering choosing my next words wisely, but before I could rebuttal, a knock on the window startled me. It was Derrick at that moment I felt like a damsel in distress and he was my hero. Clearly it bothered My Uncle Richard, because happiness was not on his face when he saw Derrick, however, I didn't care but Uncle didn't put up a fight he just unlocked the door and I was out of there. Hearing him speak while walking away "remember don't make me do it for you." The latter of his sentence scared the crap out of me.

"You okay?" Derrick asked me, but there was no need to put fear in his heart also because of my psycho uncle.

"Yea I'm good thanks."

"Your brother told me you would be out here." Yep leave it up to Michael to spill the beans, but this time I was actually grateful for his big mouth.

He walked me to class and he was gone. I actually felt naked without him, so I couldn't wait for lunch. If I could stay in science with Mr. Miller all day that would be awesome, but since I couldn't, I had to force myself to enjoy English, Social Studies, and math. Some days at school felt slower than others, but today was not one of those days. In the lunch room having so much fun it is filled with laughter and familiar faces. For a moment, I forgot about all the other stuff that was going on in my world. I shared with Derrick the colors of the dress, so he had an idea of what to wear. Today I actually hated for lunch time to be over because of the fun I am having. Enjoying myself so much losing track of time and it was time to go. The best part about it I only had science and gym which are my favorite classes.

Mr. Miller greeted us very cheerfully at the door today is the day we worked on our planet project. Mr. Miller divided us into groups and each group had to create the solar system with no help from him. He just provided all the materials. My group was pretty decent they all wanted to help with something which made it easier. We each colored our balls with food coloring until each planet was accounted for. The project was going to take more than one day, so we had plenty of time to work on it.

Swimming was always my highlight of the day, so I didn't mind gym class at all. It will be much funnier if everybody was out of shallow water than I will have more people to swim with. I remember when I used to feel uncomfortable taking a shower in front of the other girls, but as time went by, that feeling passed. In gym class I have been preparing for my first swim meet and I'm nervous as heck about it, because I want to come in first place. They tell me practice makes perfect, so I've been practicing hard and listening to Ms. Jones' advice.

After school, Derrick and I decide to walk to the park on this sunny day. It is the best day so far of spring had me wishing it was really summertime, but before we made it to the park we stopped and bought some ice cream. Chocolate ice cream is my favorite and Derrick had strawberry. We walked and talked the entire time until we made it to the park bench and it felt good just to escape recent events in my world with Derrick.

"Sunshine, what's on your mind?" Darn that little thought of recent events gave me away.

"It's really complicated and I wouldn't even know where to begin."

"You can tell me how gym class was today or you can tell me what just had you staring off in space?" laughter took over.

"Excuse me, what if you tell me why you are watching me so hard?" Pushing his arm.

"Crystal I can't make you talk to me, but when you are ready to talk I'm here to listen and I'll always be here."

Alright it was enough of the mushy stuff and it was time to have some fun. Finishing the last of my ice cream, tag your hit. Hitting him taking off running like a bat out of hell. Derrick chased me through the swings and around the slide. When I felt like he was about to catch me, I ran over to the bench. We ran in circles at least three times before he got smart and jumped over the bench falling and pulling me down with him. The next thing I knew he was on top of me and I was under him. Looking up into his eyes it was like I was seeing them for the first time. I never noticed how the sun made Derrick's eyes look a lighter brown and I'd never been this close to him with nothing between us, but space and heavy breathing. The vibration of his chest was an indication we are closer than close. With his hand behind my head catching it from the fall.

"Crystal are you okay?" Sounding sweet and concerned I quickly gave a response.

"Yea." Replying pushing him off me.

"I'm really better now that I can breathe again."

"Ha ha ha you have jokes."

"Something like that."

We got off the ground dusting ourselves off and Derrick even helped me take out the woodchips that decorated my hair; it was a mess. We sat back on the bench and talked. He was sharing stories and so was I just not the big one plaguing my life right now. I couldn't even allow that to be a topic of discussion. I guessed we were all talked out, because we decided it was time to head home. I have to admit I haven't had this much fun without my sisters and brothers in a long time. I mean it's always fun with Mika, but with Derrick something was different. I don't know maybe I'm over thinking something again. Back at home everybody appeared to be pretty occupied. Knowing my momma is in the kitchen, because the aroma of food that greeted me at the front door. I followed my nose and met her in the kitchen.

"Hey beautiful what's cooking?"

"Food, what do you think?"

I heard the amusement in her voice by her response. Sometimes I knew me and my mom are just alike especially when it comes to me being sassy with our mouths. She was calm and sweet, but if push came to shove, she will chop you up and spit you out with her mouth and still love you the same. That side of her we didn't see often, but we know it's there.

"How was school?"

"A drag as usual."

"Sunshine I don't get it, as smart as you are, you make school sound like the worst place that was ever created. How is Peter, I mean how is Derrick?"

No she didn't just ask me about Peter even if she didn't try to it still happened, so since she asked I may as well answer accordingly.

"Peter I don't know how he's doing because I haven't heard from him. Uh I mean Derrick is doing just fine." Placing her hands on her hips about to let it rip, but I saved myself the lecture.

"You know what momma; I couldn't agree with you more school has to be the worst place ever created."

"Girl get out my kitchen and go get ready for dinner. Can you check on the twins? See if their okay, because they are quite."

That was my cue to exit the kitchen. The twins were in their cribs listening to some cartoons that were singing on TV, so I guess they are good. On my way to my room passing the couch I couldn't help, but to think of Uncle Richard and his evil ways. In my room I did my homework while listening to the radio. My momma was right about another thing. I really didn't struggle in any of my classes and never have. Sometimes I even help Cherish and she is the senior. Speaking of Cherish, she is at my door smiling.

"Can I come in?" She didn't even let me answer she just straggled in.

"Sure come in sit down." She was already sitting with the same stupid smile on her face.

"Girl what's wrong with your face and why haven't you stopped smiling yet?"

"You are looking at the face of a girl who had her first kiss."

Everything in me was like ewe gross, but seeing how happy she was, I refused to rain on her parade. Closing my school books and giving her my undivided attention sitting on the bed next to her.

"No, when, where and how?"

Are the first words to exit my mouth and she answered in that order. I could not believe what I was hearing and a little piece of me was actually mad, because it wasn't me only in my dream I was asked for a kiss. I guess if I was the one to dance with a boy first surely she can have the title of kissing a boy first.

"I guess my kiss beats your first dance." Cherish is so giddy I couldn't even get mad at her last statement.

"Sunshine seriously I'm really sorry about you and Peter." Wow! First my mom brings him up, now her.

"What do you mean? There's no need to be sorry." Placing my arm around her shoulder.

"It's just that I know you really like him, but for whatever the reason is you're not going to act on your feelings concerning him."

She was right I wasn't going to act on what I am feeling for Peter. Bringing Peter up automatically placed Uncle Richard at the fore front of my mind. I still haven't have found out what his connections are with Peter and why does he care if I talk to him. My mind was going into overdrive and I was not ready to be exhausted mentally so early.

"Come on Cherry Berry it's time for dinner."

Following my lead as we made our way downstairs. I started to feel nervous because I didn't want to see my favorite Uncle sitting at the table again. To my surprise, he was not here just us. The twins are sick so they weren't at the table tonight but sleeping for now. I hated when anybody was sick in this house, because of two reasons. One, we all will have to do extra around the house and secondly, whatever the sickness was it spreads like a wildfire throughout the house.

For dinner we are having spaghetti and garlic biscuits which are the bomb. I wanted to bring up Uncle Richard so bad just to see a reaction from my daddy. Knowing in my heart there is more to them besides them being brothers. Earlier watching my daddy interact with Uncle Richard it appeared he was forcing himself to have a conversation with him. I know he thinks no one saw it, but I peeped it out. Well here goes nothing.

"It sure was a surprise to see Uncle Richard this morning and he was kind enough to take us to school."

I know that my tone is playful, but I am serious as a heart attack and daddy knew I was. My mom was looking quizzical and daddy instantly stopped moving. Everybody else continued eating. I started to wrap a string of spaghetti around my fork. Feeling my daddy's eyes piercing through my soul and it felt like he had x-ray vision seeing right through my intentions. It was too late to take my statement back now.

"Yea Sunshine it was and he really should come over often, so family won't feel like a stranger among family."

Momma is cheerful like her usual self, but I saw by the wrinkles that lined up in daddy's face. He was not happy with that idea.

"If he wasn't so busy doing what he was doing he probably could." Michael chimed in on the conversation.

"What does he do for a living anyway?"

I guessed that was the question of the hour and hit a nerve with my daddy. Now his red skin color was starting to match the wrinkles in his face.

"Alright, no he will not be over here and what he does for a living is not our concern. Drop it now."

Slamming his hands on the table the whole room was quite. His voice was burning with anger and frustration and I've never seen him so full of emotions. We all jumped being startled by the cries of the twins from the other room. Momma remained cool calm and collected while excusing herself. We knew she was going after the twins. The rest of us ate in silence for the rest of the night. It is so quite at the dinner table we could hear a needle fall when it hit the floor.

I made plans to help clean up afterwards plus try to talk to daddy just to make sure he was okay, but my plans came to an end when I was sent upstairs with everybody else. I didn't dispute it as much as I wanted to but I just simply gave into their instruction. Which had me believing they were about to have a serious conversation that I probably wanted no part in.

Upstairs, Brittany is in the shower, Michael is in his room ironing his clothes; something he doesn't do unless momma makes him and Cherish is looking at a magazine at her desk. It was my time to visit her domain. I slightly knocked on her door just to get her attention.

"Hey Sunshine come in."

Flopping on her bed knowing before leaving her room it will be a good chance Cherish will know everything about everything, but what I didn't know was if it was a good thing for her to know.

"What's on your mind?"

"Thinking about daddy, I've never seen him so angry."

"I know me either, but I wonder what that was all about?"

"That's the thing Cherish, I believe I know."

Turning and looking at me from her desk with deep concern and compassion in her eyes, she eventually joined me on the bed.

"Sunshine what makes you think that?"

"It's true." My voice was sounding croaky I had to clear my throat by coughing before continuing to fill her in.

"Uncle Richard has been threatening me, because of Peter." Staring at me in disbelief, she shook her head no.

"No way Sunshine."

"Yes Cherish, twice! Once over the phone and when he took us to school."

"But why? Is this why daddy was so upset? Did you tell him about the threats?"

"Of course not, but get this, when I told Uncle Richard I would tell daddy he threatened him also."

I saw the fury in her eyes and wondered if I should stop or perhaps I've already said enough. Placing her hand on the side of her head.

"Now what does Peter have to do with any of this?"

"His daddy Peter Jackson was arrested a couple of years ago." Before I could answer, she interrupted hastily.

"You mean underground Peter Jackson?"

"Yep that's him, so you have heard of him?"

"Yes I remember that case, because it kept momma and daddy arguing all the time, but Michael and I never knew why and you and Brit didn't pay it no mind. I still don't get it?"

"See, it makes no sense Cherish."

Shaking my head, I was becoming flustered at this point, because unleashing this information and I still didn't have an understanding of this situation.

"Come on." Grabbing my hand forcefully dragging me with her to the desk where her laptop was placed." Standing next to her and watch her work.

"What are you doing and what are you looking for?"

"Bay City public records."

I can't believe what I am seeing. The man on the screen looks exactly like the Peter I know, but he looked older his features were more developed. It gave me an idea on what to expect when Peter gets older I guess and I liked what I saw. We read Peter's case and we found out he was in prison for murder and stolen money and drugs, but no connections yet to Uncle Richard.

"Come Cherish we have seen enough we know what his daddy did, but we don't know what our Uncle has to do with any of this."

"You're right Sunshine, but I bet you Peter knows."

Shaking my head no, because I am not going to ask him. Then he would know I looked up his daddy information.

"Sunshine I can't make you, but if uncle is threatening you, this situation is more serious than we think.

"Girls what are you in here gossiping about?"

It was Michael and he was in a happy mood as his voice is vibrant sitting on her bed. Whatever Cherry and I was discussing is over. One, Michael talked too much we both knew that and secondly, at the moment he didn't really need to know.

"Sure come in and have a seat on my bed."

Sarcastically Cherry informed him, because Michael had already made himself comfortable by kicking off his house shoes and throwing his legs over in her bed. A sight you didn't see every day. Cherish and I looked at each other before we stared at him and he is still smiling.

"Okay what's with this goofy smile?" I had to ask as I couldn't resist, plus he is making it so obvious.

"I really don't want you gossiping bunnies in my business, but since you asked. I have a date for the dance also." Cherish and I laughed and joined him on the bed.

"No seriously. Pleading his case.

"Okay who is the lucky girl?"

Cherish beat me to the question. Michael pretended to fix his imaginary tie, cleared his throat and spoke.

"Judy said yes? Really?" Cherish and I was in harmony like a church choir.

"I don't know why you both are acting like her saying yes to me is unbelievable?"

"It's not that Mikey, we are just surprised because it's Judy."

Cherish attempted to help me, because the last thing we wanted is to make Michael feel he didn't deserve her. If anything, she didn't deserve to attend the dance with my big mouth and big hearted brother. I'm usually not a fighter, but if she hurts him she will hear from me.

"I wrote her a letter first and told her if she was interested to meet me after school and she did."

Whoa I can't believe what I am witnessing, we all had dates. Starting to feel tired so I made my exit peacefully and said my goodnights. Thinking about Peter even more, I couldn't get him off my mind. Telling myself to call him. Making my way downstairs finding my daddy on the phone the way he is tensed up I knew it was serious and it made me wonder who was on the other end of the phone.

Suddenly feeling a sharp pain in my stomach thinking it is Uncle Richard my head started to spin. Doing a U-turn back upstairs, but daddy snapped his fingers getting my attention pointing to the couch for me to sit down. Obeying and waiting until he was done. He ended the conversation with "protect my family and thank you". Now I really am concerned something is going on more than we knew. Hanging up, I had his attention it is uncomfortable, because he is intimidating unintentionally.

"Yes daddy." My voice came out as tight instead of relaxed how I wanted it to be.

"I know I told you Peter was trouble, but that is not all the way true and I should trust you to make good decisions."

This had to be a dream and I am waiting for something to wake me up, but I didn't wake up, he kept talking.

"I'm sorry Sunshine about Peter and exploding at the dinner table. I made a mess of everything." He got up to walk away jumping up as fast as I could and hugging him. Wrapping my arms around him as much as his wide body allowed me too.

"Daddy thank you and I love you, but this is not your fault, so please don't blame yourself." He said nothing but kissed the top of my head and he was gone.

Sitting on the couch feeling excited about the news my daddy just shared with me about Peter. Maybe if he had this revelation earlier it could have been Peter I'm taking to the dance. Not taking anything away from Derrick, he is my best friend, so I planned on having fun regardless. My fingers couldn't dial Peter's number fast enough. Come on answer the phone chanting while being impatient and he answered finally.

"Hey Peter are you busy?

"Hey Crystal yea what's going on?" Crystal really? I'm going to ignore that.

"I wanted to tell you as soon as possible my dad gave me the okay when it came to you."

There was the longest pause ever and I couldn't believe the pain I was feeling behind his silence.

"Oh, well I think it's really too late for his blessing now and I think it will be best if we didn't talk anymore."

I am convinced my heart is pleading, but realized it was the pool of tears flowing from my face onto my chest. He couldn't mean this. Why was his tone so harsh towards me?

"Peter what? Why? You don't mean that? I know I didn't want to sound desperate or pathetic, but I couldn't help it.

"Crystal I meant what I said and it's not a good idea, so please lose my number and act as if we never met, bye."

Standing here in shock for a moment before really understanding what had happened. When reality kicked in I realized I was dumped by a guy who I never agreed to be in a relationship with. Being a ball of emotions hurt, angry, and confused, but the feeling of being hurt stood out the most.

Running upstairs to take a shower hoping the water will wash away my tears, but it didn't help me, I actually cried more trying not to sob. After the shower standing at the sink staring at the steam that was on the mirror. The tears were not showing my eyes no mercy the last time I cried like this is when Grand mom Betty passed. Wiping the steam from the mirror revealing my reflections and I cried even more. Having so many questions, but the main one is why? Meeting my gaze in the mirror and noticing my eyes started to swell and they are red. I knew they would be bigger in the morning and I figured I will blame it on my allergies. Staying wrapped up in my towel sitting on my bed reaching for my journal.

Dear Journal,
Words can't really express how my heart feels right now. I've never felt this way before and the worst part about it is I don't know why Peter decided not to talk to me anymore. Maybe it is my smart mouth, my judgmental overprotective daddy, or my psycho Uncle. I'm not sure, but the one thing I am sure of is that this is a hurtful feeling and I want for it to stop.

PETER

I knew I had to tell Crystal we couldn't talk any more. I want to protect her as much as I could and if not communicating with her is a way I was going to make it happen. I was glad she called me it is always a pleasure of mine to hear from her, but I hated that she was hurt at the end of our conversation. It was the right thing to do especially after meeting up with my daddy and learning more about Mr. Evil. He is going to pay, but I don't know how yet. I just knew he couldn't get away with hurting people, especially those I love and cared about. It hurts my heart to know Crystal is hurting, but I had to keep reminding myself it is for her own good.

I wanted to call her back so many times tonight to make it right and tell her everything I knew, but it would only further endanger her and if something happened to her because of me, I couldn't live with that guilt on my conscience. Feeling trapped because I have no one to talk to. My mom was asleep and my daddy was miles away and I couldn't pick up the phone to call him. I prepared myself for bed which I am sure I wasn't going to get a lot of sleep, but I am going to try.

CRYSTAL

My eyes were sore from crying and I could barely see. I saw three silhouettes and all of them appeared to be recognizable. When finally realizing who they are, fear settled in my heart. Why is Peter and my daddy having coffee with Uncle Richard and they are laughing? Approaching the table my daddy was the first to greet me with a long endearing hug and I was lost in the love he has for me. Followed by a handshake by my Uncle I was hesitant because I didn't want to be nowhere near him and I really didn't want him touching me. Last but not least, I am embraced by the boy who just dumped me. Peter whispered in my ear that he is sorry and everything will be alright. Pulling myself back away from him, anger started to fill my heart and tears started to flow again. I wanted to punch his face for making me hurt the way I am hurting.

"Crissy please don't cry, I said I'm sorry." Wiping the tears from my eyes his voice is full of concern, but I was too stubborn to be sucked in so quickly. I snatched my face away.

"Crissy please don't fight me." He pleaded.

"Don't tell me what to do, you are not the boss of me do you understand me?" Pushing my finger in his chest so hard that I felt the pain shoot through my entire hand.

"You win." He threw up his hands smiling.

"Come on."

He took my hand following him away from my daddy. While we were walking I felt him tensing up beside me which made me start to worry instantly. When he pulled me closer to him and I knew something was up.

"Crissy, when I say run I need you to run like your life depends on it."

I had no time to reevaluate what is said to me, however, I was ready to comply. The next thing I heard was the two loudest bangs and people were screaming. Over the screams I hear Peter scream run and I took off. Running right into the arms of Uncle Richard. How could this be when I left him at the table, but if he's here, where is my daddy? Are questions I thought about and panic begins to take over. I turned back towards my daddy with a gun to my head. I see my daddy on the floor motionless and I couldn't help him. Screaming daddy as loud as I could it was hopeless because he was not responding.

"Let her go Rich she knows nothing and it's me you really want."

My tears are flowing like a river and I have no control over them. Wanting to get to my dad motionless body, but his grip was too tight to even move. Being close enough to smell his after shave and the coffee he had been drinking.

"I hear you kid, but all she had to do was listen and stay away from you, so since she didn't, it must end this way."

Hearing a click and the gun is pressed even harder into my head. Peter charged towards me but before he made it, shots are fired. I screamed while watching Peter's body fall to the ground. Being released dropping to my knees and crying out Daddy, Peter, but neither one responded. I looked up and noticed Uncle Richard was out of sight. Sitting there rocking back and forth in a pool of tears. Feeling a touch on my shoulder from the back. I screamed and woke up to Brittany. She said nothing, but hugged me and I cried even more on her shoulder.

CHAPTER 7

That night I cried myself to sleep. Nights turned into days, days turned into weeks and weeks turned into months. I still haven't heard from Peter and this is the longest it has been without any form of contact from him. I have tried to pop up over Pat's house but still nothing and the only thing Pat will tell me is "maybe next time". My sisters, my momma, and my best friend started to feel sorry for me because they are treating me extra special. I am getting used to the extra attention, but I am a Hartland and nobody's charity case. They say time heals all wounds, but after this I think time allows you room to adjust to change.

I finally made it up in my mind that I will no longer feel sorry for myself and no more pity parties. Wiping the last tears from eyes fighting through my feelings, because what I really wanted to do is get back in bed and hide under my covers. My swim meet was today and I worked so hard for it and I refuse to miss it because of boy problems. Dressing myself, fixing my hair in a messy bun and I even put on make-up nothing much. Some Cherry lipstick and eyeliner. I checked the mirror and gave myself the okay, grabbed my bags and made my way downstairs.

"Good morning my beautiful family."

Interjecting getting everybody's attention and all eyes are on me. I felted like a star in my own house that was being admired by thousands of adoring fans.

"Look mommy, Sunshine is pretty." Tanisha noticed my make-up and everybody smiled.

"Good morning baby."

Hugging me only my mother's voice can be so endearing and captivating. Leading me to my spot and we all ate breakfast pancakes, eggs, turkey bacon and orange juice all of my favorites.

"I don't know why she put make-up on knowing she is going to just cry it off anyway."

"Michael shut up."

Daddy's voice was hard and sharp, and if this was a month ago Michael would have been right, so I wasn't going to fight. I had cried so much these last week's I thought I was going to run out of tears.

"Daddy it is okay I'm good and for the record big mouth Mikey, no I'm not going to cry my make-up off thank you very much."

Sticking my tongue out at him as humorous as I sounded, I am serious. Big booty Judy and big mouth Michael is a big perfect match after all for the dance and who knows, maybe a relationship also. Daddy and Michael found him something to wear regardless of what had transpired between Peter and me. I am going to have an awesome time at the dance and plan on winning my swim meet. I had to change my focus, so I could continue to pick myself back up and go after the things I wanted before Peter. Realizing what is important to me.

"Sunshine are you ready for your swim meet?"

"Of course I am daddy.

"Are you scared?" Brittany asked me.

"A little, but I'm scared of losing also, because working so hard that I don't want to let myself down."

"Sunshine you shouldn't be so hard on yourself."

I know my daddy is right and I shouldn't be so hard on myself, but sometimes I am my own worst critic.

"Don't sweat it Sunshine you are the best in the school, you got this and besides it will be like taking candy from a baby."

Finally Michael said something that made sense, and he is right. I am the best in our school, but what about my competition from the other school? I guess I will find out later today.

"Momma please don't be late today."

The meet started at 5:00pm sharp and I don't know when I will be up, so I didn't want my family to miss me. I wasn't coming home after school, so I wouldn't be here to help my momma be on time. That's why I'm stressing the time to her now.

"Baby don't worry about that we will be there and on time, so Michael, Brittany, and Cherish come straight home." They all nodded their heads in agreement.

"What about you daddy will you be there?

I still haven't told anybody about my awful nightmare when Brittany found me the next morning in a pool of my tears. Thinking about it made me feel sad all over again. Daddy must have seen the sadness on my face.

"Sunshine don't look like that, of course I'll be there."

Only if he knew this look was not about him being absent from my competition, but being absent from my life. I gave him a weak smile and a nod. After breakfast we are off to school. While walking out the door, momma hugged me tighter and whispered in my ear that everything will be fine and she loves me. I felt assured that everything will be okay.

In school, Derrick is waiting for me and from the expression on his face I can tell he is memorized by my make-up also. He made me consider if this was a good idea wearing this make-up. I hated being the center of attention.

"Hey Derrick what's up." Appearing to be in a trance he just stared at me and said nothing left me smiling.

"Uh hello? Earth to derrick." I tried to snap him out of it.

"Crystal I'm sorry you just look so different. Pausing and staring some more. "But different in a good way."

"Come on, let's get you to class."

Using his words on him, we laughed and headed to our classes. After separating from Derrick I felt alone again. Why do I feel so secure around him? I gathered a lot of stares today and even got the attention of Stacey. For a minute, I thought she was going to say something to me, but she just rolled her eyes and went her way. The teachers even took notice to this make-up. Mika would be so proud and when I see her she's going to be surprised. Wondering if she will be here today at my swim meet on time. I'm in need of all the support I can get. They have been so supportive throughout me being dumped for the first time and if it is up to me, it will be my last time. Thinking about me being dumped made my stomach hurt all over again.

"Hey Sunshine guess what?" Looking around to see who called me and it is Mika and I am elated to see her.

"Hey lady." Throwing my arms around her like I haven't seen her in years. She held me back in front of her and examined my new look. I can tell she is pleased.

"Awe Sunshine look at you. You look so pretty." Placing her hands on her mouth.

"So, what's the good news?" I asked, taking the attention off of me.

"I know what you are doing, but I'll let you pass this time. I went to my counselor and asked if I could switch my lunch she said yea, so now we have lunch together no more sneaking."

This is fantastic news now my best friend will be dining with me and not just my sisters, I couldn't be happier. We walked to lunch with Derrick he was surprised to find out the news also. The lunch room was chaotic everybody had a conversation going on. Treading light on the food as I didn't want to eat real heavy, so I wouldn't be sluggish. The first conversation at our table.

"My girl Crystal's going after that medal today."

Derrick's confidence in me is inspiring he made me believe I could accomplish anything. Derrick has always been supportive, especially during the preparation for this swim meet. Knowing he will be there cheering me on is comforting. I think Derrick is my number one fan.

"That's today?"

Mika asked with a look of disappointment. I couldn't believe she forgot about one of the most important days of my life. I was speechless, but I'm sure my emotions were written all over my face.

"Sunshine stop I'm just playing girl you know I didn't forget about your big day. Plus I get a chance to see Elmer High School swim team." Punching her shoulder she was talking about seeing other boys while talking to my cousin.

"Wait, you do know the boys are not swimming, just us girls right, but what about Pat?"

"I know now, but I bet you the boy's swim team still will be there to support, and what about him? I mean he's cool and all, but we haven't made anything official yet." The way she spitted those words out her mouth made me believe something went down between them and I missed it.

"Why what happened? I thought you guys were getting along well?"

"Sunshine we are, but like I said, he hasn't asked me to be his girlfriend yet, so that makes me a free agent still."

"Well you know there is a strong possibility he may be here this evening."

"Oh, I planned on him being here."

With a twisted smile and tucking her hair behind her ear, Mika made me think she had something up her sleeve concerning my cousin. Mika's never been dumped she is always dumping the guy, so in my eyes, it must be nice to do the dumping.

"Pat doesn't have a chance does he? Derrick interrupted. "But before you answer, does Pat know that you want to be his girlfriend?"

"He had a chance alright; his chances are just running out."

We all laughed at the way she said. It may have sounded funny to our ears, but I know Tamika, and she was serious. I'm actually starting to feel bad for my cousin.

"No, but for real Derrick, of course Pat knows as a matter of fact, it was him who brought up the conversation first about me being his girlfriend. Exactly how long does he expect me to wait on him to make a decision?"

"Tamika give him time if Pat was the one to bring up you being his girlfriend first like you said, then trust me Pat making you his girlfriend will be coming next."

"I agree with what Derrick said." Cosigning with Derrick pointing my fingers in his direction and staring at Mika.

"Excuse me who's side are you on Sunshine?"

When it comes to Mika and Derrick, Mika is always pulling the I was your friend first card to make me change my mind, but this time, there was no changing my mind because Derrick is right.

"Mika why do you always have to go there? Look like Derrick said be patient before you do anything rash and end up like me, dumped."

Dumped was more of a whisper as it left my mouth, but Derrick still heard it the only person who is clueless to what went down between Peter and me. The cat is out the bag now.

"Wait dumped? What did I miss?"

Looking at us both with so much passion and concern in his voice feeling compelled to give him the rundown, but not now, I didn't want to be distracted today.

"Yea about that, I promise we will talk, but just not now."

Placing my hand on his shoulder. The lunch bell rung it was time to go. We all went our separate ways, but before I went to class, I stopped in the office to see my counselor. I wanted to make some changes concerning my classes next school year. I wanted to keep swimming, however, I just wanted it earlier in the day and I wanted the same teacher.

"Ms. Brown." I muttered knocking on her door. Looking up at me smiling her always chipper self.

"Hey Ms. Hartland come in, have a seat. What's going on is everything okay?"

"Yes everything is fine. I just wanted to make some changes in my schedule for next year." She gave me a smile that indicated she was surprised.

"Crystal don't you think it's too early to be making plans for the following year?"

"No actually, I don't this is the thing Ms. Brown. I want to keep my swimming class I want Ms. Jones and I want it earlier in the day especially since I'm about to win this swim meet. I must keep swimming, because swimming may be the key to get me a scholarship for college."

"Crystal, what makes you think you're going to win?"

"Because Ms. Jones and I practice really hard to prepare me, so losing is not an option." The sound of the bell ended our conversation, but before I left out her office.

"Ms. Hartland, I will see what I can do."

Nodding my head in agreement walking out thinking it was better than a no or that there was nothing she can do. In science, my group project won the contest on the solar system and was picked to be on display, so today we set it up in the front hallway of the school. I am proud and happy, because all of our hard work paid off. We all received an A on the project also.

For some of my group members, it was their first A of the class and we are at the end of the school year. Feeling bad for them yet happy because I was a part of this achievement with them. When we were done, we all did a happy dance being silly congratulating one another. Finally, making it back to class everything appeared to be normal. We have been doing a lot of recapping preparing us for finals. I am ready for finals also thinking I am on a roll and ready to face anything that came my way.

Making it to gym class everybody is excited you felt the excitement in the room even from those who weren't participating in the meet. Ms. Jones is more firm than usual, especially on those preparing for the meet. We worked harder on our techniques and strategies. Ms. Jones felt like some kind of swim camp drill sergeant instead of a high school swim teacher, but I guess giving the circumstances Ms. Jones had to be hard on us.

After class I met up with my sisters and brother just to touch base with them and to make sure they were going straight home like momma instructed them to. Derrick decided to stay after with me, I stressed to him he didn't have too, but he insisted so I didn't argue with him. He helped me with some stretching exercises while waiting. I can honestly say he came in handy after all, but I must admit it was weird having him so close to me at times. I knew if I felt the weirdness he felt the same thing, but we never said anything. It was 30 minutes before the swim meet and now I'm nervous.

"You okay Crystal? Please don't say you are when your face is saying something different."

"Nope I'm not for the first time I'm feeling nervous and I'm not sure if I'm ready." Hanging my head down.

"Crystal, look at me you got this and you have no reason to feel any other way but victorious."

Raising my head up to meet his gaze. Derrick's confidence in me was breathtaking and his confidence left me speechless, or I am speechless because he is touching me. This is no time for me to become a ball of emotions, I shook it off quickly.

"Thank you." Whispering in his ear while giving him a hug.

"No problem Crystal that's what I am here for to be your friend."

Our hug is interrupted by the guests who started to fill up the place. Coach gathered all of her swimmers together, took us in the back before I could see the arrival of my family. In the back, she gave us some more pointers and a victory speech. Ms. Jones reminded us on how hard we all worked and we all are winners in her book.

We made our way back to the pool area and I saw the bleachers are packed. I instantly started to look for my family. They spotted me before I found them. I saw my mom waving hysterically. It is comforting to see them, but when I didn't see my dad it made me sick to my stomach and my mind started playing tricks on me. *What if Uncle Richard got him somewhere, or what if he was in a car accident*? I had to pull myself together and fast. Focusing on Derrick's words it gave me courage to keep going.

I learned that the 100-yard freestyle will be after the two 50-yard breaststroke races. Which is alright with me and it gave me time to keep preparing myself mentally. It is time to start hearing the instructor give the commands while the swimmers are doing some last minute stretching on the board. But when she yelled on the mark, everybody went down like a set of dominos. The buzzer went off and they had emerged into the water.

Watching and cheering with anticipation really for both teams, because I knew we all practiced hard. I am tickled by Elmer High's choice of colors swimsuits. They are orange swimsuits with lime green swim caps which made me appreciate our red and black. Bay City took home a medal and Elmer high took one too. Brenda must be proud of herself especially since she is the one who caused us to win during the breaststroke race.

It is my turn up on the board looking up towards my family and there he is, my man of steel. My daddy made his arrival and he was giving me the thumbs up. I said a little prayer that only I could hear and when I heard on your mark, I was down and ready. The buzzer went off and I was gone giving my best strokes and hearing my name being called muzzled through the water was motivation. Touching the end of the pool and making my way back not really paying attention to who's behind or next to me. I kept my eyes on the prize. Swimming my last lap touching the pool indicating I am done and realizing I was in first place and set a record for speed. The crowd went wild and I felt overwhelmed with joy. I looked around barely able to see clearly and in the crowd, there was Peter. Wiping the water from my eyes to look again, but he was gone, maybe it was the chlorine causing my eyes to play tricks on me.

Getting out the pool, my teammates met me with hugs and handshakes while we all waited on the judges to make the official announcement like they did the 50-yard winner. When my name is called to receive my medal, that's when I realized I actually won. In the locker room, coach congratulated us and shared with us how proud she was. We showered and got dressed. Back in the gym room people were waiting to shake our hands and have a picture taken with the team. I was in disbelief because I just wanted to be with my family and I am not used to all this attention. Having to admit it did feel good to be in the spotlight for the first time. Making my way through the crowd, I finally made it to my family and they are as excited as I am.

"You did it." Michael ran to me picking me up and twirling me around.

Going down the row hugging and kissing everybody, by the time I made it to my momma she was already crying tears of joy and she made me cry. For the first time in a long time they are tears of joy instead of sadness.

"You two break up the crying session Sunshine I am so proud of you baby girl." Giving me a bear hug, my daddy has the best hugs.

"Cousin Girl I was scared for a minute I thought somebody had kidnapped your body, because I couldn't believe that was you out there swimming so effortlessly." Leave it up to Pat to talk trash hugging me and being so close to him, I couldn't help but to think of Peter.

"How is he?" I whispered while he is still close to me so no one could hear me.

"Girl don't be worrying about that knuckle head, but nevertheless he is holding up he told me what happened finally and it's been no walk in the park for him either, but enough of him. What's next for you?"

"School next year." I muttered smiling and plus, I knew Peter was okay.

"Excuse me Crystal."

Came from behind me and knowing it wasn't family, because all my family is in front of me. Turning around to see Stacey and her entourage. I immediately got an attitude on one of the happiest days of my life I have to deal with pretty Stacey. Making it up in my mind regardless of what she is about to say she will not take me off my cloud nine.

"Yea what's up?" I said, replying nice as possible.

"We just wanted to congratulate you and I was wondering if you will take a picture with me? I couldn't believe what I was hearing is she serious? Do I have fool written on my forehead? Stepping back bumping into Cherish getting her attention.

"Sunshine is everything okay?" She asked after she evaluated the scene, but before I could answer, Stacey beat me to it.

"Yes big sister we are okay. I just wanted a picture with Bay City's new Champion and I hope it's not a problem?" Coming from Stacey.

"What do you say Sunshine?"

"I really don't know Cherry."

"It's only a picture and besides you can't tell your adoring fans no." Stacey was right, I didn't want to tell supporters no, because they actually came to the swim meet, but I wonder why she wanted this picture.

"Okay sure." With a heavy sigh I agreed. Stacey even allowed Cherish to take the picture, but before she snapped it, Cherish applied some cherry lip gloss on me and rubbed the kinks out my hair.

"Perfect." She muttered before snapping the picture and she gave Stacey back her phone. Stacey looked at the picture and declared with a jubilant voice.

"Awe Crystal we are so cute." Showing me viewing it and agreeing with a thank you.

"Okay Crystal I won't take up any more of your time, thank you for the picture again.

She and her goons walked off like nothing ever happened and I was happy they were quite the entire time, because I really didn't want to deal with them anyway. It was bad enough dealing with Stacey looking around to see everyone engaging in conversations. Seeing Mika and Pat talking and from the way it was looking, Mika was getting what she wanted. All of a sudden I'm in the air over Derrick's head staring in his eyes. That was shortly lived, because my daddy broke that up quickly and I was actually glad he did. This was the perfect opportunity to properly introduce my date to my dad.

"Dad, this is my date for the dance Derrick Lester."

"Nice to meet you mister Hartland as Crystal's date." Derrick announced while extending his hand out for a handshake. *Please daddy don't be rude thinking to myself.* My momma must have seen the same thing, because she interfered.

"Hi Derrick, I'm Miss. Hartland and it's our pleasure to meet you also." She spoke while pushing my daddy in his side. It was funny to see when he wanted to be tough he couldn't around momma, because momma had a way of breaking him down sometimes.

"Yea what she said." Shaking Derrick's hand firmly.

"Alright who's ready for Pizza?" Momma shouted, my stomach was agreeing with her. Breakfast was cool and lunch I didn't eat that much just enough, so I have officially worked up an appetite.

"Me." Yelling loud trying to beat everybody again.

"Pizza it is." Momma was still excited it was all in her voice and I was happy to know I played a part in her being excited. Looking over at Derrick, I wondered if he wanted to come eat with us. We had three cars, so we had more than enough room to share. Plus he did stay with me today and was here for me, so it was only right that I personally gave him an invite.

"Hey Derrick do you want to come eat with us?" He was looking surprised.

"Sure of course, but I hope it's not a problem?"

"Daddy it's not a problem is it?" Shaking his head no and I laughed even harder on the inside. I knew I got my stubborn ways from him. I am my daddy's child in so many ways. It was so much fun having everybody here who I cared for. Sitting at the table surrounded by loved ones full of happiness. I was starting to feel unhappy though, thinking about everything that happened from my break up with Peter, my project winning the science contest and my victory in the pool today. I would think these things alone would be enough for me to be happy because my good outweighed my bad, but the hurt in my heart is saying something different.

"Sunshine don't look so sad; Peter will come around."

Words from my best friend giving me a wink. Smiling and thinking about what Pat had said and maybe Peter misses me as much as I have been missing him. The outing was spectacular and it was so nice to be around everybody. I really hated for our gathering to come to an end, but we had to go back to our lives.

When I was home, I was exhausted I didn't stay downstairs to chat with the family. Knowing my body will be sore in the morning, I decided to soak in some muscle therapeutic bubble gel. The smell of mint filled the bathroom and the scent is relaxing alone. I almost fell asleep in the tub for the first time. I guess I was more tired than I thought. As much as I wanted to sit and enjoy more, I knew my bed was calling my name. Plus I didn't want to look like an old raisin when I looked in the mirror and gross myself out. I put on my favorite pajamas that were so big my body got lost in them. Just the way I liked my clothes.

Sitting on my bed feeling fresh and smelling good, my name was called telling me someone was on the telephone for me. My heart almost jumped out my chest thinking of who could it be on the phone. In my mind, I wanted it to be Peter, but it my common sense, I knew it wouldn't be. Making the journey to the phone felt like I was on my way to find out my fate. I was experiencing so many emotions and I had to pull myself together before reaching the phone.

"Hello." Speaking hesitantly.

"Hey Crystal, it's Derrick, and your brother gave me the number I hope that's not a problem, but I was just calling to tell you again how proud I am of you and I'm really glad that we are friends."

This was a strange yet pleasant surprise out of all people who it could've been in my head, Derrick never crossed my mind.

"Thank you Derrick, I really appreciate you for being a friend and thank you for all the encouragement you have given me."

I couldn't believe he had me smiling so hard. Ok, this is starting to feel weird.

"Alright that's all I wanted plus, you need your rest and I'm sure you're tired."

Why was he trying to get off the phone with me so fast? I must have had some kind of free pass for the phone. My parents could have easily shut it down especially when they knew Derrick wasn't family, so I planned on taking full advantage of talking on the phone. It wasn't a problem for him to have my number, well not now at least.

"No Derrick, you don't have to go yet we can talk. I'll get some rest trust me."

Pleading my case to Derrick in my most convincing voice. It must have worked, because we stayed on the phone for a good hour talking about everything. Derrick shared his dream of owning his own company in welding if going pro didn't work out and I shared my dream of being the owner of a school or some form of a childcare center.

Dear Journal,
Today was a great day. Tamika now has lunch with me and I won my first swim meet. I also tried something different today I wore make-up to school and everybody loved it, even me. If I started to wear it more I would have to adjust to the attention that comes along with it. I'm tired, so I'm about to answer my bed calling my name. Oh, I was even glad to hear Peter is okay.

PETER

Sitting on my bed thinking about these last two months and all that has transpired between Crystal and me. Since my last conversation with Crystal, I have felt heavy in my heart and I thought by now it would have changed, but it hasn't. I know Pat is tired of me talking to him about his cousin, but he's my best friend and at the moment the only person I'm sharing my feelings with about girls. My mom knows about them, but I never just admitted my feelings about girls bluntly to her. Since speaking to Crystal last, I have fought with myself so many times, such as should I call her? Should I go see her? Those questions filled my mind faithfully. I called myself having an idea allowing Pat to be my mouth piece, but it still will lead back to me, so that was a bad idea.

When Pat told me about her Swim Meet I knew I had to be there, so when time came I found myself hiding in the shadows of the crowd. Crystal may have not seen me, but I saw her to the very end and when she won I was gone. Trying my best to avoid being seen making my great escape, but bumping into Stacey and her crew. I made up a story that I knew she couldn't look into, but yet it was believable even to me. Convincing her to take a picture with the winner and sending the picture to me, so I could have a picture with her standing next to the winner. Actually feeling bad when I asked, because I really just wanted a picture of Crystal and she was more than happy thinking I wanted the picture for her, so maybe I was wrong?

When Stacey sent the picture to my cell phone, in that moment, I was glad she had my cell phone number and she did as I asked. Now I could see Crystal at any given moment. When I saw her on the picture, I paid no attention to Stacey all my focus was on Crystal. She looked happy and radiant basking in her moment of victory even if it was taking a picture with pretty Stacey. I know she worked hard for a medal, and I'm sure she deserved to win.

Staring at her picture having a strong urge to just call her and tell her everything, but knowing that would only put her at risk so I tossed that idea away. I was tired of going in circles when it came to this entire situation with Evil Rich. It was enough of me thinking about everything that was out of my control. Deciding to think about the upcoming dance. I needed to practice on my dance moves. Turning on some music and danced until I got the attention of my mom.

"Boy what is all this noise going on in this room?"

Asking after storming in my room knowing I had disturbed her, but it was too late she was in here now, as a matter of fact, she may as well dance with me. Grabbing her by the hand twirling her around letting out a girlish scream while dancing with me. We danced and we danced. We owned my bedroom floor and we had fun.

"Baby, momma is not as young as I use to be."

Flopping on my bed catching her breath with her hand over her chest, so I knew she had reached her limit.

"Okay momma, but at least you don't look as old as you feel."

Leave it up to me to try and keep a smile on my favorite girl's face. Every time I try I succeed, so it is worth it. She deserves to smile.

"I take it you're getting ready for this dance in a few days?"

"And you will be correct." Joining her by flopping on the bed next to her.

"Mom I plan on dancing the night the way."

She laughed, but the problem is, I wasn't being funny I was being serious. I gave her my I'm serious mom face and she got on board with it.

"Sweetheart I'm sorry, you can dance your little heart out if you choose to, so I hope the shoes you bought are comfortable." Giving her my accepting smile.

"Well baby I'm going to let you continue doing whatever you was doing, but I'm about to call it a night." Kissing my head before she left the room.

Admiring her strength and courage it gives me strength to believe we will be okay. After dancing up a sweat, it was time to smell fresh and clean. Preparing for a shower wrapping the towel around my waist. Looking in the mirror at my six pack pleased that it started to form and it showed me all my hard work running and crunches are paying off. I'm having a proud moment examining my body.

Fixing the water to hot and almost unbearable is the only way I can take a shower. The average person couldn't take my showers, but I wouldn't have it no other way. Steam and the aroma of old spice Fiji filled the air. The hot water was relaxing but the soap gave it an extra push to relaxation. My run in the park was pretty intense, so a shower and relaxation was very welcoming to my tired and beat up body. When all the hot water was gone, I knew it's my cue to get out the shower.

Sitting on the bed after putting me some pajamas on and feeling relaxed, refreshed and clean. My mom and I haven't heard from Rich in a few days maybe this is a sign of him leaving us alone. The sound of my phone vibrating took me out my thoughts. I immediately thought what if it's Rich calling, but my mind was put to ease when I see it's Pat.

"What's up Brother?" Was the first thing I said when answering the phone.

"Hey man chilling just got back from hanging out with the family."

"I guess I didn't get the invite?" Being comical, because I knew I couldn't go even if I wanted to.

"You got jokes I see, but anyway I wanted to tell you that Sunshine was okay and she won the swim meet." I heard the excitement in his voice about her winning, but I had to act surprised as he couldn't know I was there either."

"Really?" In my most surprising voice.

"Yes dawg she did great and she was really fast, it was my first time seeing her swim. I had a proud cousin moment when they announced her as the winner."

"Man that is fantastic news and thanks for sharing it with me." It was quite between us for a minute which felt awkward.

"Anytime Pete I know one thing, I wish you two get it together and fast, because you're making each other crazy."

"Crazy how?"

"She's asking about you and you over here lighting up like a dear in headlights with just the mentioning of her."

"Did you say she asked about me?"

"Well yea she did and I told her the truth."

"What truth is that?"

"I told her you turned into a crybaby and I never seen you cry so much period, not even from a whooping from your momma." I was feeling bewildered I couldn't believe he told Crystal I was over here moping around. I don't care if it is true she didn't need to know that.

"Pat please tell me you didn't?"

"You're right I didn't she just asked if you were ok and I simply told her that you are okay and this hasn't been a walk in the park for you either.

"Man, Pat you play too much." We both just laugh it was a much needed laugh.

"Whatever fix it and fix it quick, before you lose her."

Wait hearing lose her repeat in my head sent a sharp pain through my stomach, which penetrated my heart. What did he mean? Did he know about evil Rich and was he after her now?

"What is that supposed to mean?" Trying to keep my tone down, because I didn't want to disturb my momma again or alarm him.

"It's just tonight her friend Derrick was there and they were almost looking like a couple, but you know, looks can be deceiving. I'm just saying brother if you like her like you say you do, show her."

"Alright man thanks and I'll see you tomorrow."

Pat hung up and I was left with all my emotions, but there was no way I was about to stay up and ponder on Derrick or Crystal. I'll figure something out and soon. Falling back on my bed feeling my eyelids become heavier, sleep has called my name and I answered happily.

CHAPTER 8

PETER

I woke up feeling refreshed wiping crust from my eyes. I threw my legs on the side of the bed. I walked to the bathroom, and I noticed something is different the smells of eggs, pancakes and turkey bacon wasn't floating in the air. Quickly shaking the sleepiness off myself, I started quickly running to my mom's room calling her name, but I got no answer finding her room was empty. Looking for her in the library she wasn't there either panic or fear; maybe both filled my heart. Finally running to the kitchen no surprise the kitchen is empty also. I called her cell phone and could hear the phone ringing in the house which led me to start searching for it. When I found it I went through it. I looked for calls out of the normal in her call log and no calls from or to Rich. I made my way back in the kitchen sitting at the table about to call Pat. The house phone rung and I answered it before even realizing I was out the chair. The other voice on the phone was music to my ears it was my momma. Hearing her voice calmed all my fears.

Learning she was okay I was able to continue my day. She woke up late and didn't have time to cook breakfast, so I had to settle with cold cereal. After grabbing me a banana out the fruit bowl, I was on my way. Making my way to Pat's house he was walking out the door smiling when I was walking up.

"What's up brother from another mother?" Pat spoke.

"Hey man, you ready?" High fiving each other.

"Let's roll."

We walked to school as usual. The breeze was great and the sun was shining. I knew summer was closer, but it felt closer than months. The winter weather wasn't bad either I was still able to run at the park during the winter season, so that was a plus for me. The winter season for Bay City usually makes you feel we lived in Antarctica. In the past, we experience Snow Mountains for days and the cold air was beyond freezing, but Mother Nature had spared us and I am grateful for more than one reason.

"You ready for that dance?" Pat bringing me out my thoughts and back to the conversation.

Truth be told, I wasn't sure if I still wanted to go, but it was too late to cancel on Stacey and it wouldn't be fair to her. But I did not want to see Derrick and Crystal together it wouldn't be safe for him.

"Man I'm really not feeling going to the dance anymore. At first it sounded like fun, but that was before Crystal and I stopped talking completely."

"I knew you not wanting to go had something to do with Crystal, but don't let her stop you from having a good time bro, besides seeing you there she may have a change of heart that night. Think about it, her seeing you there all dressed up looking good and seeing Stacey on your arm. She's bound to feel some kind of way."

Pat may be on to something, but I didn't want to make Crystal jealous. I've seen that side of her before and I didn't like it much.

"Okay she will feel jealous and she will have no reason to be, because I like her not Stacey, and plus she doesn't know I'm coming."

"Another reason for you to be there."

Laughing, at least he was finding humor in it because I found none.

"You wrong man laughing at me."

I punched him in his arm.

"Okay enough about us, what about you and her best friend?"

"Oh, that's easy she's my girlfriend now and she's going to the dance with another guy which is driving me crazy." My turn to laugh.

"Bro did you say girlfriend? When?"

"Yes I did and the night of the swim meet we made it official."

I'm happy for him. I've never known Pat to have a girlfriend. Pat always talked to girls, but to actually label one as a girlfriend never happened. I have had my share of girlfriends and Pat met everyone that I know of. Staring at him with amusement on my face.

"Don't look at me like that, because she is my first girlfriend I thought it through and she is different from any girl I've met so far." That statement left me speechless literally.

"You know how most girls can be forward and blunt, she is the opposite and I like that about her bro."

"Well if you like it, I love it."

I mean who was I to rain on anybody's parade? Especially when it came to relationships, because I was clearly making a train wreck of a relationship with a girl who was never my girlfriend. The more I thought about it, the more it became funny, which caused me to laugh out loud.

"Why you laughing?"

"Man you don't want to know." Shaking my head. I mean, it makes no sense to keep repeating myself when it came to his cousin.

Finally arriving at school, it appeared to be a full house, and before I could get a rebuttal from Pat for not telling him what was funny. We are interrupted by Sarah and her crew. I have known Sarah ever since preschool, her mom and my mom used to catch the bus together before dad bought us a car.

"Hey guys what's up?"

Even though she said guys addressing us both, all her attention is on me intertwining her arm in mine and it made me think about what Crystal said at Pat's party. This was no time for her to express her feelings and Pat must have seen it also and he came to the rescue.

"Dang girl let the boy breath. Give him some space."

The words had already left his mouth while breaking her arm free from mine. I was shocked, because I'd never seen Pat so aggressive not even playing basketball and it left me wondering what that was all about.

"See bro, this the female I was talking about earlier; forward and blunt."

"Whatever."

Sarah said smacking her lips pushing me like I said the statement. Pat and I both laughed as she walked away. We went to class and the day went by fast. My favorite class is gym, because I love basketball and wrestling. It was actually pretty jacked up that the freshmen had to pin us before they moved up in rank on the wrestling team. Sometimes we would go easy on them, but the ones who really thought they could pin us we showed no mercy. Coach Walker is the best; he pushed us to do our best in everything we did. Some students think he is a jackass, but I take it as tough love. Today I was planning to jog straight after school, but I changed my mind due to me working extra hard in gym class, my body was already tired. Pat will sometimes go with me so he is surprised to find out I wasn't going. Honestly, I just wanted to go home eat and chill. My mom was making my favorite steak and homemade mash potatoes.

The walk home was quite, I guess we both are tired plus Pat and I did a lot of talking this morning on our way to school. On the way back home, we walked with a crowd, because there are a lot of kids who live the same way. Their conversations are intriguing, but I did not have the strength to indulge in them. I laughed and agreed with most of their conversations.

Finally, making it home walking through the door the aroma of fresh steak and seasoned potatoes greeted me first before I even saw my momma. Making my way to her library, because I knew that's where she will be. Just like I thought, she was there balled up in her favorite recliner chair reading and she looked like she already showered because she had on some house clothes.

"Hey my beautiful momma." Getting her attention taking her eyes off her book.

"Hey son, how was school?"

"It was ok I guess. Oh, my last game for the year is coming up, so make sure you're there."

I really didn't have to stress her being there, because she never missed a game no matter what.

"Well, I will see what I can do."

Sarcasm, I guess I deserved it and it was another reminder of how much I act like her. Dinner is fantastic and I enjoyed every bit of the food. The steak is tender it melted in my mouth and the potatoes are seasoned just right. My stomach was rejoicing because it was satisfied. We were both quiet for the most part; a lot of the conversation's answers are yes and no on both ends. We talked about dad and planned a day to go visit him, the date was set in stone. We planned to go see him after the dance after we send him pictures so we can discuss them on the visit. When I was done with my dinner, I worked on my homework and then decided to chill around the house for the rest of the day. I thought about calling Pat to see if he wanted to chill, but then I thought about his new found status having a girlfriend. I decided to hold back on that idea, so he can give her as much time as she needed and wanted.

CRYSTAL

The time has finally come, tonight is the night of the dances and everybody is excited. We all went to school and it was about time that things felt normal again, well before Peter. My emotions are more stable and my thinking is clearer without the extra emotions from liking Peter. Derrick appeared to be ready for tonight hoping I didn't let him down finding out my dancing sucks. This made me wonder if I should tell him now or let him find out tonight, but knowing I didn't like the element of surprise, I made the choice to tell him while walking home from school.

"Hey Derrick, look there's something you should know." He paused instantly and curiosity filled his face.

"What's up Sunshine?" Perfect, now he has completely thrown me off. He's never called me Sunshine before and now I'm curious to why he's calling me sunshine, but anyway I can't worry about that now.

"I don't know how to dance." Trying not to sound as sad as I probably was looking.

"It's a dance and you don't know how to dance?" He was laughing.

"I'm glad you are finding me funny right now." I said with my arms folded and rolling my eyes.

"Before you go postal on me, hear me out first. I'm not going to the dance with you because of your dancing, but because I wanted to be seen with the prettiest girl in school."

I was about to give him an ear full, but decided not to chew his ear off bowing out gracefully.

"Ok if you say so?" Making my response short and simple and not giving away any emotions even though I knew my face is red from blushing. I couldn't believe Derrick is having this effect on me and I'm not sure what to make of Derrick. I knew he liked me and if I'm honest with myself, he always has liked me. I never viewed Derrick as anything but a friend, however, now I can actually feel that changing. I guess not seeing or hearing from Peter made paying attention to another boy easy. Peter was out of sight and out of my mind, well sometimes at least.

We continued to walk home and when we made it to my house; we went our separate ways until the dance. Brittany is so excited you'll think she's going to the dance and had a date. She is actually trying to give me and Cherish some pointers and she is the youngest. Her advice sounded logical, but I really couldn't take her seriously for at least one main reason she has never been on a date. I knew about her fan club of boys at school, but it wasn't enough. The boys at school are crazy about Brittany I don't know if it's her caramel skin, pretty teeth, dimples in her cheeks or her outgoing personality, but whatever it is, they really like her.

When we finally made it home, I'm overjoyed to see my auntie with all her equipment for our hair. Yes she is going to have us looking gorgeous. As soon as we stepped in the house it was show time. We have less than five hours to be ready and out the door. Mika went home to take a shower and she came back over in some boy shorts and a shirt. She didn't have her dress because she wanted to get dressed at home because Pat is at my house and she didn't want him to see her. When her hair was finished; she went back home to get dressed.

When I got out the shower Michael and daddy made it home. I met them at the front door and Mikey is looking good with his fresh haircut with his zigzag lines on the side of his head. Mom wasn't so thrilled about those, but she didn't make a big deal of it.

I was the last one to get my hair fixed and to take a shower. We all had an up do hairstyle that complimented our personality. Mika has a silky swooped pin curled with shiny rhinestones and red streaks, Cherish has a slick backside bun with a roller coaster bang, and I have a straight pin curled up bun with highlights, light brown mixed with my cocoa brown hair. We will definitely be turning heads tonight, however, I wish that all of us were going to the same place. Enchantment under the sea will be at the school and one night only will be downtown at Bay City Renaissance Hotel, the best one in the city.

It was that time and my nerves were getting the best of me trying to keep my cool in front of everybody. Cherish and I came downstairs and all eyes were on us, even Michael stopped adjusting his tie to look at us. My man of steel was pleased with our looks as he twirled us around together admiring our dresses. A knock on the door interrupted our session of excitement for a moment, because when Mika walked through the door it started again and everybody was in awe. We took so many pictures before our dates arrived, and after. I had to admit even Michael's date Judy looked fabulous in her pink and silver mermaid dress.

Cherish' date drove them to the dance and my daddy took us in a rented all black suburban with chrome wheels. We were going to pull up in style. When Derrick saw me for the first time at the house, he stared for at least two minutes, but it felt like the longest five minutes of my life. I could tell Pat wasn't so happy with Mika and her date, but Pat kept his cool. Poor James probably didn't even know he was standing in the room with his date's boyfriend. How Mika managed to pull this off I may not know tonight, but later I will be asking questions. When the finishing touches were applied to our faces, it was time to roll out.

Pulling up to our destination Derrick was out first opening up the door for me, and James did the other side for Mika. Michael rode with Judy and her family in their red corvette pulling up behind us. We all said our goodbyes to our parents and it was time to make our entrance to the gym.

The gym had a complete makeover and we were all amazed. The gym walls were no longer brown and tan, but blue water wall paper and chandeliers out of clear air bubbles coming from the ceilings. Fish and dolphin lanterns are hanging from the ceiling also. The icing on the cake was the sunken ship photo booth and the cherry on top has to be the clear grown sized sculptures of mermaids that filled the gym. The decorations left us in awe and almost speechless that it was our gym, but the decorations had us feeling like we are under the sea. No complaints from me, everything is beautiful the blue actually complimented mine and Mika's dresses. Mika wore her tulle opened which showcased off her stunning legs and her laced straps that are going up her leg. I wore mine closed, but you could still see my slippers.

We stood around in a group for a minute, but that didn't last long because when an upbeat song came on, we were on the dance floor dancing and having fun. Lord knows I was just moving from side to side like I was in church acting like I knew how to dance. Catching Derrick laughing at me a few times when the music stopped, he asked.

"Crystal, would you like something to drink?"

"Sure." Muttering.

Derrick walked towards the punch and I went the opposite way to find a table to sit at. I spotted Mika and James taking a picture in the sunken ship, she looked gorgeous and happy. The sparkle in her eyes said it all. Everyone looked pretty darn good. Suddenly, everyone's attention is on the entrance. I could barely see myself I just knew whoever was getting all the attention had on white from what I could see. Standing up to get a better view, I had the wind knocked out of me seeing who it was, I fell back in my chair holding my stomach from the pain it is feeling. Pretty Stacey and Peter. I felt so many emotions hurt, angry, betrayed and ironically feeling relieved also, because it was really good to see Peter and how fine he looked tonight.

I wanted to walk over and speak to Peter, but my pride wouldn't let me move. Gazing around to find Mika, but she is into her date and was not paying attention to nothing else. Derrick brought my focus back to him handing me my punch that I no longer had a taste for. I was starting to feel sick to my stomach needing to go to the ladies' room.

"Crystal, are you okay?" I was so tired of hearing that question after hearing it so many times over these last few months it was starting to become irritating, but not wanting to take my frustrations out on Derrick.

"Yea I'm fine; I just need to make a trip to the ladies' room." Derrick didn't fight me he just obliged.

Excusing myself, I went in the direction of the ladies' room. While walking, Peter and I made eye contact and there's something in his eyes I have never seen, but I kept on moving. In the restroom, I was wetting some paper towels in cold water and dapping it across my forehead, because I'm burning up and sweating. Giving myself a pep talk before leaving out the bathroom looking in the mirror I was ready to continue enjoying the dance with my hot date.

The bathroom was on the outside of the gym which was a plus, so all eyes wouldn't be on me coming out the bathroom. Opening the door, Peter is right here in my face. My heart and feet froze in place. Peter pushed us back in the ladies' room and locked the door behind us. At first, I was afraid thinking about my daddy's warning, but realizing there's no reason to be afraid.

"Peter what are you doing?" Keeping my voice low rolling my eyes and stepping back from him.

"Crissy we really need to talk; there's so much you should know."

Stepping closer to me until I'm pinned up against the wall and him. The smell of his curve cologne made me weak in the knees. I'm familiar with curve, because my daddy and Michael wears curve. With his arms on each side blocking me in the warmth of his minty breathe which threw my thinking completely off. I was being held in his captivity against my will and secretly loving every minute of it so far. Peter looked good, his high cheek bones made him look older, Peter smelled like a fully grown man and his voice sounded almost as deep as my daddy's. Catching me admiring his lips.

"Okay, start talking then Peter, because I think you forgot we both have dates out there probably wondering what's taking us so long."

"Dang baby girl you are looking beautiful tonight." I know that's not what he wanted to talk about I see him hesitating but why? This might be serious?

"That's it? If so thank you, but I really have to get back to the dance." Folding my arms over my chest and for a split second, his eyes were there on my chest.

"Crissy I've missed you and that attitude." Peter muttered with laughter.

Trying to move, but him having me stuck in his presence is intoxicating and I don't know how much more I can take before my emotions get the best of me.

"Crissy, your Uncle Richard is not who you think he is."

My mind went back to Cherish conversation we had in her bedroom. Cherish was right, Peter knows more about Uncle Richard than I thought. I really didn't want to mess up my night with a conversation about him of all people.

"Come on Peter I'm really not in the mood to discuss my Uncle and his evil deeds tonight."

"You're right, but I refuse to keep going on like I don't miss you or want you around, so after the dance will you call me when you get home?" Giving me a smile that met each corner of his face which made it hard for me to say no.

"Yea I guess I could." Sounding nonchalant.

"You can act like you don't care, but I know the truth."

Peter is right, I cared and I cared a lot. Maybe more than I should. Perfect now he's staring at my lips.

"Can I kiss you?"

No he can't be serious what about Derrick and Stacey?

"Uh I don't think pretty Stacey or Derrick will like the idea of you kissing me."

"Girl, who cares what they think at this point? I don't, do you?"

"Duh yes, I care unlike you I actually have a conscience and care about other people's feelings Peter."

"Too shay is that what you think, I don't care about people's feelings?"

The next thing I knew his lips are on mine and I'm following his lead. Closing my eyes and giving into him completely wrapping my arms around his neck. I couldn't believe I am actually kissing Peter. This was not right, it had to be wrong because it felt so good. I was starting to think about Derrick and how he would feel knowing his date is in the ladies' room kissing Peter.

"No, Derrick this is not right." Pushing him off me forcefully.

"You just called me Derrick, but I get it, so I'll forgive you this time because I care about your feelings."

"Alright can we go please?" Irritated and excited all at the same time.

"After you beautiful." Stepping out the way clearing a path for me.

Telling him to wait a minute before walking out after me was a good idea, because as soon as I opened the door Derrick is right here waiting for me which made me feel horrible again.

"Derrick" Muttering startled and embarrassed.

"Yea I had to come check on you and make sure everything was alright.

"I'm better now, you ready?"

Leading him far away from the ladies room locking my arms up with his. Mika met us at the table.

"Girl, I was wondering where you two disappeared to?"

If only she knew it was me who disappeared and Derrick just came to search for me, such a horrible date I am.

"What's wrong Sunshine? Never mind, dance with me."

Pulling me to the dance floor leaving James and Derrick behind to watch from a distance. Sharing with her everything that happened between Peter and she pulled me closer. I couldn't believe her reaction, but this is Mika I'm talking to with a date and a boyfriend at home. James and Derrick joined us on the dance floor interrupting our dance. We danced to a few upbeat songs and everyone appeared to be having a good time. Everyone had smiles and laughs, creating memories that will last a lifetime. One slow song came on and Derrick pulled me closer to him and I watched Peter do the same with Stacey.

Laying my head on Derrick's chest, taking in his strong, masculine, heavy, manly and distinct scent. Peter was the complete opposite, his was smooth and alluring scent that added a sex appeal about him, nevertheless they both smelled great to my nose and I had no complaints in the department of body odor. I was feeling safe and comfortable in Derrick's arms, probably more than I should have. After the song went off, we went to get something from the food section of the room. They had salad, fruits, baked chicken, mash potatoes, green beans and mac and cheese. All my favorites, so I got a little of everything not caring about what Derrick thought about me eating all this food.

Back at the table, we sat and ate Derrick and me, Michael and Judy and Mika and James. We talked and we laughed and shared stories about the ending school year. Of course being the winner of the swim meet came up thanks to Mika and all the attention was only on me which made me blush. I mean, they are really doing the most reliving my moment of victory. Standing up clapping and bowing down like they're in the presence of a queen is amusing and it got the attention of Stacey who was making her way to our table.

"Hey Guys what's up, doesn't everyone look wonderful?"

Hearing and witnessing the sincerity in her voice and on her face. With Peter on her arm, I was becoming annoyed at the sight of him on her arms, but for the first time, what I was feeling did not show on my face and I decided to remain nice.

"Hey Stacey you look marvelous also."

She really did a white mermaid dress with a sweetheart neckline and a small train. It was a dress fit for a bride. Peter never took his eyes off me giving me butterflies in my stomach and apparently Derrick noticed him staring at me, so he got Peter's attention.

"Peter right?" Reaching his hand out for a handshake.

"Oh, where are my manners?" Stacey muttered, but it is too late now.

"Yep that's me the one and only." Why is he so arrogant around people? Peter shook Derrick's hand and kept the conversation short.

"Well it was nice talking to you all let us continue to enjoy ourselves tonight."

The last words Stacey said before walking off and Peter said nothing but nodded his head. Mika stared at me and I knew what she was thinking shaking my head no.

"Come on Crystal let's go take us a picture to capture this night."

Standing to my feet and Derrick was leading us to the sunken ship. Feeling so hypocritical standing there with Derrick with his hand around my waist wanting it to be Peter's, and for a minute, I imagined that it was Peter taking pictures with me. Yep Derrick killed that thought though, but not intentionally.

"What you think?" Showing me our pictures. We looked good almost like the picture perfect couple.

"Yes I love them." Hugging him.

"And I love you."

Derrick whispered in my ear, it was like an alarm went off in my head sirens flashing red lights the whole thing made my head spin. Tensing up and stiff as a surf board, I froze in his arms. I was quiet and Derrick literally dragged me back to the table and sat me down.

"I'm about to go mingle and won't be far away if you need me."

Giving him a weak smile while he was walking off. I watched him walk away pretending he just didn't tell me he loved me, but I know maybe I'm over thinking again placing my head on the table full of questions and concerns. I even thought about what Peter said in the bathroom, my Uncle is not who we think he is. Would my Uncle really hurt us? Answering my own question, yes, I believe he will. It is sad to think your own blood will hurt you, but he left me with no choice. Raising my head up to distract me from my thoughts and the intro to a song came on. I recognized the song and it was placing me back in my cousin's basement. The song Peter and I danced too. Laying my head back on the table sighing and now my thoughts are in over drive.

Feeling a tap on my shoulder, I was waiting to respond thinking

it was Derrick because I really wasn't ready to face him right now, but hearing the voice calling my name and feeling a tap again I knew it wasn't Derrick. I gazed up to Peter's smiling face.

"I think their playing our song." Extending his hand to mine.

"I didn't know we had a song?" Placing my hand in his.

Peter led me to the dance floor and pulled me into him. I was looking around to find Derrick and I found him dancing with Stacey. Laughing because I knew Peter arranged that hook up. Looking over Peter's shoulder at Mika, she was giving me the thumbs up. Placing my head on Peter's shoulder thinking this night is perfect now and nothing can bring me down off my cloud nine.

"Sunshine, you know I really care about you girl."

"Yea whatever."

He stopped dancing, maybe he had enough of my attitude pulling me away from him and staring in my eyes. He finally gave me a half smile that said he was up to something.

"Okay, if I didn't care would I do this?"

Peter kissed me in front of everybody and honestly I enjoyed it because I didn't stop him. When he stopped kissing me, I was back in his arms listening to Bobby Brown Roni. I wonder if Peter is going to love me for the rest of his life. The next thing I knew, he started to sing and I was falling in love with him.

"Oh, so now you're a singer?"

"Nope, it's one of my favorite songs and I'm dancing with my favorite girl."

Peter was putting it on thick tonight it almost felt like we never stopped talking. I'm back in his embrace enjoying his warm and alluring scent. Peter twirled me around and to my surprise, I spotted my Uncle Richard and fear instantly crept in my heart. Stumbling back into Peter. Peter looked up to view what spooked me. Uncle Richard is coming towards us with a bat in his hand and he wasn't by himself. The other man is short and a very muscle bound man with his gun drawn out on the crowd. Everybody was screaming and scattering. Was my Uncle coming for me or Peter?

There was a stare off before words are spoken.

"You just didn't listen Sunshine, so now I have to make you stay away from baby boy Peter."

Tears flooded my face like hurricane thinking about our encounter in his car and his warning. I looked into Peter's eyes and he didn't seem bother at all just fearless. Peter placed his hands in the air in a surrendering position and spoke.

"Leave her out of it Rich, it's me you want."

"See that's where you're wrong she has everything to do with it. I told her to stay away from you and here you two are together. What a lying witch of a mother you have." Even though Uncle Richard is calm, the hostility could be heard in his voice.

Those had to be fighting words, because the next thing I see is Peter charging towards my Uncle and Peter socked him in the face. It wasn't hard enough to make him fall, but stumble. Wiping the blood from his mouth laughing.

"Is that all you got?"

Peter tried it again, but was stopped by the man with the gun. He hit Peter with the gun and Peter went flying across the floor. I was screaming and running to his side as he just laid there with no movement. Jumping up to face my Uncle, because he is strolling our way knowing I couldn't beat him and I wasn't going to try.

"Uncle please don't do this I'll stay away from him I promise." My voice is barely a whisper, but my words were understandable.

Grabbing him hugging him trying to give Peter some time to get up, but he just tossed me to the side like a bad habit. Uncle Richard is hovering over Peter's lifeless body looking down at him.

"You see Sunshine; this is what happens when you don't follow my instructions."

Uncle Richard raised the bat and began to beat Peter repeatedly like he wasn't even a human. Peter screams in pain and left me feeling hopeless, because I'm watching and there is nothing I can do. Then the voice of a savior came from behind me and I was elated to hear my daddy's voice.

"Drop the bat Richard, come on man that's a kid. What are you thinking?"

"Daddy."

Screaming as loud as my lungs allowed me to. He already had his weapon drawn proceeding towards the madness. I tried to run to my man of steel, but I was snatched up by the gun man placing the gun to my head and he said nothing the entire time. Uncle Richard let Peter have it until Peter was silent again and at that moment, I was thinking he is dead. I screamed his name, but no answer no sign of life. Uncle Richard started laughing and anger filled my heart.

"You monster."

I yelled and the gunman gripped me tighter. Staring at my daddy connecting his eyes with mine and nodding my head. Indicating I was about to do something crazy, but he didn't know what. Never taking his eye off me. Remembering the heel on my shoe, it wasn't long, but it had a sharp point on it. Raising my foot and stomping the gunman's foot with all my might and he tossed me to the side like a rag doll letting out a scream of agony. Pointing his gun at me, but before he fired, I heard the loudest bang I've heard in my life and the gunman lay on the floor. I couldn't even scream as I stood in shock.

"You witch."

Looking at his hit man on the ground, my Uncle yells while raising the bat coming towards me falling on the floor screaming daddy loud as I could. There is that pop sound again and my Uncle's lifeless body is lifeless next to me as his blood started to flow next to my shoes. Scooting back frantically away from him and his blood. I mustered up the last strength I had getting up and I ran into my daddy's arms. Sobbing in his arms he just held me.

"Sunshine baby I'm so sorry are you okay?"

"Yea, but daddy what about Peter?" Muttering with a shaky voice.

Daddy released me and we ran to Peter's side as he lay lifeless on the gym floor.

Peter laid there unresponsive and I was crying non-stop. My daddy handed me the phone and instructed me to call 911 while he administered CPR. Informing the operator on everything that took place, everything went black before passing out on the gym floor. Feeling like I was in a deep sleep, I heard my daddy's voice, but I couldn't respond.

The next morning, I woke up to a lot of beeping sounds, cords and monitors hooked up to me. I noticed the white walls realized I'm in a hospital bed. Looking over and seeing my mom sleeping in a recliner chair.

"Mom."

Whispering because that is all that I am able to do. My throat burned even when I opened my mouth, but she heard me and she jumped up so fast and came to stand at my side with tears in her eyes.

"Don't speak baby the doctors said your voice needs plenty of rest."

The way my throat felt I'm not going to fight those instructions, but there is so much I needed to know. I pointed to a piece of paper and pen next to her purse on my food tray. When she gave it to me I started to write.

Where is Peter?

She paused in her movement and I saw all the dreadful emotions on her face as she tried to avoid my question. I wrote again.

Tell me where is Peter momma? Please I need to know.

Finally, she gave in and told me everything and she left me lost for words literally. My heart broke when she told me Peter was in a coma with swelling on the brain and it may take weeks or months for him to wake up or not wake up at all. I wrote her another note.

What's wrong with my throat?

"The doctors said it's vocal cord hemorrhage, but you should be fine with rest and observation, so for a couple of days you will be here then you can go home."

Home is sounding good right about now, but then again, any place will be better than here. I rubbed my stomach indicating I'm hungry. She quickly grabbed my food off the tray and started to feed me. The warmth of the soup felt good going down my throat, so I ate it all. There is a knock on the door that got our attention. Walking through the door was my man of steel. After kissing my momma he asked.

"How is she?"

"You know our baby is a trooper like her daddy."

"Hey my Sunshine." Placing his hand on my hand and noticing my notes to momma.

"I see you've been asking questions." He muttered and looked at me with amusement. Nodding my head up and down.

"Well before you ask me, I'm going to tell you because I know you want to know. Uncle Richard and his henchman didn't make it."

Tears covered my face as he kissed my forehead comforting me and I felt my mom squeezing my hand and she was crying too.

"You know Sunshine, that was very brave and stupid what you did."

Nodding my head agreeing with him, I grabbed my paper and pen.

But brave?

"Yes Sunshine brave, but don't forget stupid."

So now I'm your hero, I saved you for a change.

"Yes you did baby girl."

Laying back to rest, there is another knock on the door and it is a short haired nurse older female with salt and pepper hair. The doctor is much younger and he appeared to be Asian, but his accent and his voice said he wasn't Asian. They both checked me out. I could barely open my mouth for the doctor to look in, but he managed to see what he needed to see.

"Well parents, Crystal is as healthy as your average 15-year-old and you guys can take her home later on tonight. Her vitals are normal and I'm convinced everything was elevated because of the traumatic experience. Her throat does not require any antibiotics, but I will give her something for discomfort and pain. Do you have any questions for me?"

"What about school doctor?"

"To be safe, she should really stay at home for a week or until her checkup which will be a week from today."

"Okay thanks doctor, see you next week."

Then it was just us again and they are excited I can come home, but I have to be honest, I am not looking forward to missing school for a week. The time has come, they unhooked me and I got dressed in the clothes my momma brought for me. Making my way into the bathroom to get dressed, I looked in the mirror and I was looking horrible. My eyes are swollen and my bun that I had is long gone. Meeting my parents back in the room, I grabbed the pen and paper to write.

Can I go see Peter while we wait on my discharge papers?

"Sure I don't see why not." My momma answered before my dad.

"Sunshine take it easy on your voice please and he's down the hall room 124."

My daddy told me before I left the room, he knew me so well sometimes it scared me, because he knew I was going to attempt talking to Peter. Peter's room was easy to find especially since my room was 128. I took my time to find his room and when I found it, the door was closed, so I knocked. A lady answered the door she had to be his momma and he looked nothing like her. She pulled me in her embrace.

"Sweetheart I heard about what you did. Thank you for saving my baby and I know you can't talk so don't try to, but I know you came to see him and I will give you a minute."

She walked out leaving me with Peter and all his machines; he had more than me. I walked slowly to his bed placing my hand in his hand and tears took over my face uncontrollably. I laid my head on his bed and sobbed. I couldn't believe all this had happened to us. If I stayed away from him, this would have never have happened and he wouldn't be in this bed hook up to all these stupid machines lifeless. I placed my face on the side of his face and spoke into his ear with my hand still in his hand.

"Peter can you hear me? Please wake up, don't die on me."

It was killing my throat to even whisper, but I didn't care. I wanted for him to hear me and know I'm here.

"It's me, Crissy your favorite girl, please don't die on me"

After those words I sobbed even harder next to him and that's when I felt him squeeze my hand, but I couldn't react because one of the monitors went off and caused the nurses and doctors to flood the room. They put me out and I had never felt such hurt in my short life of living. I met Peter's momma in the hallway and I grabbed her and whispered in her ear.

"I'm sorry for everything."

THANK YOU

To my Lord and savior Jesus Christ for allowing me the usage of this gift called writing. To my church family Rising Star Ministries C.O.G.I.C in Detroit where my pastor is Superintendent Dr. Herman Davis. To my first lady Lawann Davis for always believing in me. To my father A.G. Turner(rip) thanks for loving me. To my mom Rhonda Turner thanks for raising me and showing me how to be a great mother, a friend, and a strong woman. To my siblings Stacey, Paul, Snuggles, Rosie, Vyjaus, Destiny, Edward, and Gregory. I'm truly grateful that you guys are a part of my life. To my children Xzavier, Edward and Rose you are my motivation. To my Godmother Tennessa Palmer Knox for always encouraging me. To Shevaya and Tamara for always having my back. To Angela Slater (my angie) for being an ear and a shoulder to cry on. To everyone who love and support me. I appreciate and love all of you. Thank you so much.

Love, Veronica

ABOUT THE AUTHOR

Veronica Mull is a proud Michigan resident and a woman of God. She is a mother, a friend, and a skill full writer. Her first book *Revealed* is a collection of poetry from her heart and she hopes it helps you in some way. Soaring is her first novel of many to come and if a person dares to dream. Veronica wants to inspire you to go after your dreams and soar!

www.facebook.com/Veronica-Thoughts-1005739232797012

Made in the USA
Monee, IL
31 March 2022

93566625R00094